FAKED AND FUMBLED

KNOXVILLE COYOTES FOOTBALL
BOOK 1

GINA AZZI

PROLOGUE

RAIA

BROOKS'S MOUTH is moving but I don't understand the words.

"I think we've gotten complacent." His tone is pleading. His eyes beg me to understand. To agree. To nod and smile and absolve him from the guilt he's feeling.

But I'm in shock.

"Complacent," I test the word out. "Brooks, we've been together for a decade."

He sighs. "Come on, Raia. We were fourteen when we got together. Did those years even count?"

I shuffle back half a step as if he pushed me.

"That's not what I mean," he backpedals, but it's too late.

"They meant something to me, Brooks." I try to keep my voice even.

Behind him, the soccer field beckons. The girls on my team glance over, a range of annoyed, curious, and worried expressions on their faces.

"Of course, they did. For me too. But, Rai, we never experienced anything else," Brooks continues.

"*Anyone* else. Is that what you meant to say?" I shoot back.

His expression twists. Pain flashes through his eyes.

A day ago, hell, five minutes ago, I'd wrap my arms around him. I'd console him and coax him into confiding his thoughts, his vulnerable feelings, to me.

Now, I want to shove him away. Hurt him as badly as he's destroying me.

I force myself to stand straight. I lift my chin and meet his eyes.

But inside, I'm dying. Coldness sweeps my veins. Icy tentacles stretch from my stomach up into my chest, twisting around my heart. Nausea swims in my head and noises are muffled in my ears.

Brooks shakes the foundation my entire life is built on. His words force me to confront how flimsy that foundation is because I feel like I'm about to collapse like a house of cards.

All it takes is his ending our relationship.

Brooks Spence has been my boyfriend since my freshman year of high school. My first year of boarding school. He's been my constant, my pillar, my goddamn rock, through high school and university. Soccer team drama and high-pressure nationally televised games. Changing my major and navigating new social circles.

No matter what, I had him. I thought we were unshakeable.

Raia and Brooks. Brooks and Raia. Braia.

Now, nothing.

"How could you tell me this now?" I accuse, tears burning the corners of my eyes. I don't blink. Don't let them fall.

He has the decency to look remorseful. "I just, I couldn't wait any longer."

"I'm about to play the biggest game of my career," I remind him, gesturing toward the field. Toward my team who is now huddled together, gawking at me.

"Every game is the biggest game of your career," he says gently.

What? I straighten, pushing my shoulders back and arching my neck.

"Do you want me to apologize for that? I'm an athlete, Brooks."

An athlete who takes the game seriously and prioritizes my team over boozy brunches and late-night bonfires. Is he still mad that I left his birthday party early last month?

I turn away, rake my hands over my hair, blow out an exhale.

I apologized for that. Made it up to him by cooking dinner and buying an Armani blazer I couldn't really afford.

"Rai, after this summer, you're going to play in Europe," Brooks reminds me. "Don't you want a fresh start? Don't you want to go over there, focus on your team, on your game, and not have...this—" He pauses to gesture between us. "Holding you back."

I roll my lips together and narrow my eyes. Even though, logically, I understand his point, right now, my emotions are front and center. "I never thought of 'this' as a fucking job that tied me down, Brooks. Me and you...we were forever."

"Callaway!" Coach calls, blowing her whistle to get my attention.

Relief crosses Brooks's face and that's the final nail in the coffin. Or my heart.

"They need you," he tells me, sounding thankful.

"Yeah. And I needed you," I spit back.

"Raia, we'll still be friends," Brooks assures me.

I glare at him. Unless I'm planning to lose my entire friend group, the one Brooks and I have been a part of for ten years, the one that also includes my cousin and best friend, Anna, then yeah, we'll still be fucking friends. "Yay," I deadpan.

He squeezes my shoulder. "Good luck today. I'm rooting for you."

"Fuck off, Brooks." I shoulder check him as I walk toward the soccer field.

My stomach, previously slick with nerves for today's game, is now tied in knots at the blow Brooks delivered.

"You okay?" Coach asks as I jog toward the team.

"Fine," I clip out.

Anna catches my eyes and I note the worry in hers.

I shake my head slightly to let her know I'm cool.

I'm fine. I'm locked in. I got this.

But as I run through the warm-up, my mind is on Brooks.

The first time he kissed me at Anna's family's cabin in the Great Smoky Mountains.

The first time we had sex our junior year of high school.

The time he lied for me when Anna and I snuck out and nearly got expelled from boarding school.

Last year, when I brought up marriage.

My head is all over the damn place. Oscillating between the sweetness of our memories and the bitterness of our breakup.

Shit. *Brooks and I broke up.*

"Raia! You sure you're okay?" Anna asks as we move toward the center of the field for kick-off.

"I'll tell you later," I mumble.

She wraps an arm around my shoulders, and I lean on her for a full second. Anna and I have been best friends, inseparable, from the month we were born. Our moms, sisters, carried us together and gave birth to us in the same hospital, only three weeks apart.

She's been as much of a constant in my life as Brooks. Even more so.

"Come on. We got a game to win." Anna squeezes my shoulder.

"Yeah," I agree.

We lose the coin toss and I wonder if that's a sign of things to come.

It is.

Because two minutes into the game, a forward and I

collide head on. Pain rips through my shoulder and burns a path that cuts through my chest. My breath stops and I go down.

Hard.

"Fuck," I swear, as a wave of dizziness washes over me.

In my peripheral vision, I note Anna's horrified expression. I find Brooks on the sidelines and wince at the shock that twists his face. I close my eyes and roll over as vomit crawls up my throat.

"Hey, hey, you okay?" The referee is at my side, followed by Coach and the trainer.

"Callaway," Coach says. "Stay still."

"I'm fine," I protest, trying to push to my feet. "Let me walk it off."

Coach Williams gives me a hard, searching look. She nods and the trainer and Anna help me to my feet. Slowly, I walk toward the sidelines as clapping and cheers ring out from the crowd.

"You all right?" the player I collided with asks.

I nod. "Yeah. You?"

"All good, baby," she replies, jogging back onto the field.

As I turn to watch her, agony blazes through my side and I wince.

"You need X-rays," Coach says.

Absentmindedly, I nod. I know I need X-rays. I know I'm done for the summer.

And, perhaps most painfully, I know Europe is no longer an option. Not this summer anyway.

I just lost my team, my dream, and my constant.

In one afternoon, my life took a massive detour from the carefully laid plans I've been plotting and executing for years.

Everything I thought I knew is over.

I'm now on my own.

ONE
COHEN

THE METAL BAR rattles as I re-rack it. My hands slip and I swear, reaching for a towel to mop the sweat off my face. I upped the weight today and my body is feeling it.

"Shit, Cohen. How much time did you take off this summer?" My team captain, and oldest friend, laughs.

"None of it," I say, sitting up. "You?"

Avery Callaway, our cocky quarterback, grins. "I was hitting the gym. Two-a-days." He flexes obnoxiously. I flip him the middle finger.

"Yeah, okay," I snicker, knowing Callaway was MIA last week, having an intense sexcapade with a SI swimsuit model from the early 2000s.

Ever since his public breakup with Mila Lewis, another one of my good friends, Avery has spiraled in his romantic life.

Not that I should judge. My situation isn't much better. I date woman after woman hoping to feel *something*—a spark, a connection, a desire to want more than the moment—but it hasn't happened yet. To be honest, I'm done trying.

If Cupid wants to knock me on my ass, he'll need to send an arrow straight through my heart.

"I haven't seen you in a minute," I continue, standing.

Avery slides onto the bench and I move to spot him.

He shrugs. "Things have been hectic."

I raise an eyebrow. "Your MILF call it quits?"

He snorts. "Fuck off." He completes a set and sits up, taking a swig of water. "Nah, Raia's home."

I frown. Last I heard, little Raia Callaway was training to play soccer in Europe. That had always been her dream. Play abroad for a handful of years before coming back to the States to play and inspire little girls across the country that they can be professional soccer players too.

Hell, it's why she went to that fancy boarding school in New England. It's why she ghosted our hometown most summers. It's why I've lost touch with her over the past few years...

What would make her change course and come home now?

"Why?" I ask, dumbfounded.

Avery sighs heavily.

A prickle of unease works through me. "Is she okay?"

"Yeah, she'll be all right," Avery replies without giving any damn information.

I wait impatiently.

He takes another swig of water. "Brooks broke up with her."

My face scrunches up in confusion. Raia Callaway came home because some bougey dickwad broke her heart? "And?" I ask, knowing there has to be more to the story.

"Right before a big game."

I tip my head back and groan. I hope I'm wrong on where this story is headed. "She was distracted."

"Collided and went down," Avery confirms.

"How bad is it?" It must be pretty bad if her ass is in Knoxville and not Bologna or Barcelona.

"Broken ribs, a displaced shoulder, and a hyperextended

knee. On their own, she probably could have battled through the injuries, but all together…"

"She's out for the summer," I conclude.

"Yep," Avery agrees, laying back down to complete another set.

I spot him, noting how focused he is. That's Avery. He can push his personal life to the side and home in on football all day, every day, if he has to. Then, he can turn it off and be fully present in his personal life.

It's why he was such a great boyfriend to Mila for all those years. I mean, until he wasn't. It's why he can keep up with his playboy charades while hanging onto his family-man reputation. It's why he's one of the best quarterbacks in the country and literally helped our team earn the tagline "the Pride and Joy of Southern Football."

I don't have that capability. So, while he finishes another set, my mind whirls.

"When did she get home?" I ask.

"A few weeks ago."

"How's she feeling?"

"Hanging in there."

"And the ex?" I press.

Avery gives me a look. "Brooks was never gonna be it for her. He's a good dude but…"

"But?" I wonder.

"Boring as hell. My sister thinks she wants that prim and proper New England blue blood type, but she grew bored with him about two years ago. Right now, she's too hurt to see it, but him breaking up with her is the best thing that could have happened. Just, you know, not before a game."

"Right," I mumble.

Avery finishes his last set and I move to a different machine. I try to lock into the exercises, but my mind keeps circling back to Raia.

I haven't seen her in years but back in the day, she was

like a kid sister to me. Annoying as fuck but adorable. I knew Avery didn't care much for Brooks and to be honest, I never understood what Raia saw in the guy, but she seemed happy.

Man, it rips me up knowing she's back in town, broken-hearted and too banged up to play soccer. For an athlete, not being able to play your sport is its own kind of hell.

I make a note to drop into the Callaways' and visit her this week. Cheer her up. I don't have anything else going on anyway.

I grunt as I start my next set.

Nope, right now, I need to get my head back into the grind. Training camp, preseason, football.

There's no time for anything else. There hasn't been in years.

It's a few days before I find time to swing by Avery's parents' house. My mom requested my presence at my parents' annual tomato canning tradition. My brother, Cooper, convinced me to join him and his buddies on a day-long biking expedition.

But at the end of the week, and with training camp kicking off on Monday, I ring the Callaways' doorbell. It's funny but standing on their front porch transports me to when I was a scrawny nine-year-old and hoped Avery and Raia were home. I used to live for the afternoons when the three of us played hide-and-seek, or manhunt, until the streetlights kicked on.

"Cohen Campbell!" Mrs. C pulls the door wide open. "I haven't seen you on this porch in ages!"

"I was just thinking that." I grin broadly before kissing Mrs. C's cheek in greeting. I thrust a bouquet of flowers into her hands.

"Oh! These are gorgeous." She beams, studying the pink peonies. "Are they for the patient?"

I laugh and hold up a box of brownies. "No, the flowers are for you. I got chocolate for the patient."

"You're a good man," Mrs. C jokes.

"How's Raia feeling?"

"Besides being a pain in the ass?"

I laugh. "She always was fiercely independent."

"Right you are," Mrs. C agrees as I follow her into the kitchen. "You want a coffee? I'll let Raia know you're here."

"I'll help myself," I assure her.

While the Callaways emit Southern hospitality, I've been a part of their family long enough to make myself at home.

"Mom has jars of tomato sauce for you. I meant to bring them today, but I'll drop them off next week," I promise.

"I can pass by and pick them up. Your mother and I haven't chatted in too long and now, with all our kids in town…"

"There's much to gossip about?" I guess.

She smirks. "Raia's driving me nuts," she admits before moving toward her daughter's room. "Raia, Cohen's here!"

I chuckle as I pour a cup of coffee and kick back at the kitchen table. Everything about this kitchen is exactly as I remember. Eating Popsicles in the summertime, tossing an orange to Avery, right over Raia's head, while she tried to intervene and catch it. Doing the same thing to Mila years later, when the three of us were thick as thieves, even though I was constantly third-wheeling it.

A moment later, my childhood buddy, the one who was as attached to me as she was to her brother, leans against the doorframe.

And I freeze.

Because little Raia Callaway is all grown up.

She's wearing a pair of black biking shorts and an oversized T-shirt. Her hair is swept back from her face, twisted and secured at the back of her head with a clip. Her face and feet are bare. She looks casual and comfortable…and fucking beautiful.

"Hey, champ." I stand.

Raia winces as she steps into the kitchen, and something pulls in my chest. When I get closer, I note the fading bruises on the underside of her jaw.

I reach out tentatively and swipe my thumb over the yellow-green patch of skin. "Got you good," I mutter.

"You should've seen the other girl," she claps back.

I grin and open my arms. Raia falls into them and lets me hug her while she grips the back of my T-shirt.

"Glad you're home," I tell her truthfully.

She nods but doesn't reply. It's obvious she would much rather be in Europe, playing soccer, living her dream, than sweating her ass off in Tennessee in July.

I hold her a moment too long and am surprised she smells so damn good. Feels so damn soft. She's exactly the same and opposite all at once.

I pull away and gesture toward the bakery box. "I brought you brownies."

Raia smiles and her face opens, like a flower blooming. "They're my favorite."

"I remember," I say softly, opening the box and plating one for her.

She slips into a kitchen chair and lets me pour her a cup of coffee.

She gestures toward the hallway. "Don't tell Mom I let you serve me."

I snort and place down her mug. "Yeah? What else is new? My entire childhood was spent waiting on you hand and foot."

Raia nudges me with her bare foot and her hot pink toenails run against my calf. "Give me a break, Cohen. I'm recuperating."

"Banged up pretty good, huh?" I take a sip of my coffee.

Her hand moves to the center of her chest, and she presses there, as if holding her heart in place. I'm not sure she realizes she does it. "Yeah. This was a tough setback."

I nod, wondering if she's talking about soccer or Brooks.

But I don't ask because a part of me doesn't want to know.

A surge of protectiveness runs through me as I watch Raia curiously.

Is she pining for Brooks? Or mourning the loss of starting her soccer career abroad this summer?

Are she and Brooks still talking? Trying to work things out?

Fuck. A bead of anger pulses in my temples.

Why the hell do I care this much?

I clear my throat. "What's the plan now?"

Raia narrows her eyes. "You mean now that Europe isn't an option?"

I shrug.

"I was angling for Spain," she admits, sucking melted chocolate off her thumb.

Shit. I shift uncomfortably in my chair as I watch her. The things is, Raia isn't trying to be seductive. She's not trying to *be* anything.

And yet, I'm attracted to her in a way I shouldn't be. In a way I don't want to be.

"I'm going to heal, hit the gym hard, and go after a spot for next season with everything I have," she grits out, resolve lining her face.

I smirk at the determination in her tone. "Good."

"I'm not a quitter, Campbell," she reminds me, lifting her chin.

"Never took you for one, Callaway."

The corner of Raia's mouth turns up and she takes another bite of her brownie. "What about you? Are you ready for training camp?"

I stretch out in my chair, relaxing now that we're talking about a safe topic. Football. "I'm ready. I'm looking forward to the season starting. We've got a solid team this year."

Raia quirks an eyebrow. "And a talented rookie."

"Yeah," I agree. "West was drafted from UCLA. He's lightning fast. I won't be surprised if he breaks the record for rushing yards during his career."

Raia grins. "Are you planning to smash any records?"

I smile back. "Just my own. I was shy of 1,800 receiving yards last season. This year, I want to prove to myself I can beat that."

"Then you will," she says simply.

"You think so, champ?"

"Know so, Cohen. You're capable of whatever you set your mind to."

I dip my head in thanks. I've always had a great support network but hearing the sincerity in Raia's tone hits differently.

Her belief in my football capabilities, in *me*, is motivating. It adds to my thirst to prove myself. To be enough.

I can't remember the last time a woman had this effect on me.

I never thought it would be little Raia Callaway.

TWO
RAIA

"HEY, MRS. CASTOR," I greet the owner of the pub in town. Wincing, I manage to slide my ass onto a barstool. While my bruises have faded, my ribs are taking longer to mend. I've been home for nearly six weeks and I'm ready to start training.

Mrs. Castor gives me a sympathetic expression. "Nachos?"

"Please. Can you add extra guac?"

"Coming right up, Raia." She calls out to the cook and slides a Diet Coke with a lemon wedge attached to the rim across the bar. "It's good to see you back in town."

I force a smile and dip my head in thanks. Mrs. Castor is flagged down by a patron at a table and I exhale in relief. Wrapping a hand around my Diet Coke glass, I pull it into my chest and take a long pull from the straw.

It's not that I don't like being home, it's that I don't belong anymore. To be honest, I'm not sure I ever did. Not with Avery Callaway, Coyotes Football QB and hometown hero, as my big brother.

I've lived in his shadow from the moment I was born. Even soccer—my passion and ticket out of here—didn't put me on equal footing with Avery. At least, not in Knoxville where football is life. My athletic prowess still pales in comparison to his, as does my intelligence, wit, and looks.

I've always been second best and being back home, banged up and living at my parents' house, makes the dull ache in my chest throb. The tiny fissures of hurt that I've masked over the years deepen.

"I heard you were back," a woman says next to me.

When I turn toward the voice, I nearly slide off the barstool. "Mila!"

Mila Lewis, my brother's first real girlfriend, beams. Seeing her, some of my personal pity party fades. If anyone got the short end of the stick because of my brother, it was Mila. After years of dating, he cheated on her in a scandal that rocked our community and publicly humiliated her. Even though I was at boarding school, I heard about how Mila lost her job with the Coyotes and turned inward, shutting everyone out as she processed Avery's betrayal on top of her parents' deaths earlier that year.

But now, she looks happier than I've ever seen her. Energetic, beautiful, and confident.

Mila smiles, her blue eyes sparkling. She wraps me in a gentle hug. "It's good to see you, Rai."

"You too, Mimi." I hug her back, using her familiar nickname. "You look...amazing. Glowy."

She laughs and holds up her left hand where a diamond rock sparkles from her ring finger.

"Oh my God!" I squeal, grabbing her hand and pulling it closer so I can fawn over her good fortune. "Damn, this is huge!"

Mila chuckles.

"Your man's got good taste," I tell her seriously, dropping her hand.

"He really does," she agrees, taking the barstool beside mine.

"I'm happy for you, Mimi. Avery never would have bought you a ring that big."

We both crack up at my dig.

"For what it's worth," I continue, serious now, "I didn't speak to him for months after everything went down."

Mila waves a hand dismissively. "It's all water under the bridge now, Raia," she says, referring to their breakup. "Avery and I have made peace with things and I'm happy, happier than I've ever been, with Devon." She beams. "We're planning to move to California to be closer to his family. I adore them."

"Good for you," I say, meaning it. Even though a pang cuts through my chest because…I thought I was happy, happier than ever, with Brooks.

"How are you? I mean, despite the obvious." She points to the left side of my body where my arm curls protectively around my ribs.

I sigh heavily. "Brooks broke up with me," I admit. It should be weird for me to confide in Mila, but given the history between us—she curled my hair for my middle school dance, bought me my first mascara wand, and let me tag along to the movies with her and Avery even when he ignored me—it's not. I trust her; I always have.

"Damn, Rai." Mila looks sympathetic. "I'm sorry. And I know this won't resonate now, but do you think it's for the best?"

I snort and take another sip of my soda. "You mean, do I think Brooks is my Avery and I was just settling?"

She winces at my honesty but doesn't refute my words.

I shake my head. "I don't know. I'm too hurt to think about it logically. And angry. He said we had gotten complacent but I… Mila, I wanted to marry him."

She nods in understanding as my voice cracks.

"Here you go, love." Mrs. Castor sets an entrée-sized portion of nachos in front of me.

"Thank you," I say, pushing the dish closer to Mila. "Have some," I tell her. "I'm about to eat my feelings."

She swipes a nacho and pops it into her mouth. "You planning to stick around?"

"I don't know," I admit. "I don't...fit in here."

"Raia, this is your home."

I shake my head. "It never felt that way."

Mila places a hand on mine. "I know it was hard for you, growing up with Avery at the center of attention. But you've been gone a long time. You've blazed your own trail."

"And now I'm back, with busted ribs and a revoked contract to play in Spain," I share.

Mila winces. "Shit, Rai."

"There's always next season." The words come out monotone because I've said them so many times. People have said them to me, too. I don't think any of us believe them.

Will I play professionally in Europe? Will I get another shot?

"There is." Mila's tone holds an edge, and I glance at her. She smiles. "I'll help you rehab."

"Seriously?" Mila is one of the best physical therapists in the city. She's now a trainer for the Tennessee Thunderbolts NHL team. That's where she met her fiancé, hot shot player, Devon Hardt.

"Absolutely. Come by my office on Thursday and I'll do an assessment. We'll create a workout plan for you. I'll talk to management and Devon. Maybe I can get you a pass to work out at the Bolts gym."

"Thank you, Mimi. Truly, I appreciate it. I have a therapist who can see me in September, but I'm ready to start now. Plus, he doesn't have your experience in sports injuries."

"I'm happy to help."

"Thanks. And no worries about the gym. Now that training camp is finished and preseason has started, Avery hooked me up to use the Coyotes facilities."

"See…" Mila nudges her shoulder against mine. "Sometimes it helps to have a celebrated quarterback for a brother."

"Yeah," I agree. "He's not *that* bad." While Avery and I aren't close, we aren't at each other's throats anymore either. Since I went to boarding school, I've had a stable, although distant, relationship with my family members, save for Anna.

Mila eats another nacho. "I better get going," she says, slipping off the barstool. She waves to Mrs. Castor who passes her a brown paper bag with a takeout order. "I'll see you Thursday?"

"I'll be there. It was great to see you, Mila."

"You too. You got this, Raia. I know it feels hopeless in this moment, but you are nothing if not badass."

I give her a side hug. "Thank you."

"See you soon." Mila settles her bill and heads out of the pub.

I watch her go before turning back to my nachos.

"She's one special woman," Mrs. Castor remarks. "Your brother never deserved her."

At that, I sputter a laugh and nod. "You're right, Mrs. Castor."

Mila evaluates me on Thursday and draws up a plan to help me ease back into training. On Friday morning, I hit the Coyotes facilities to begin my rehab.

While a few of the players say what's up or give me a nod in greeting, most of the faces are new. The team has solidified in the past few seasons, and I haven't been here to watch them come together.

There's the rookie, West Crawford, that recently signed. Two new players starting on the defensive line. Save for my brother, Cohen, Gage Gutierrez, and Jag Baglione, I don't personally know most of the roster.

Popping in my AirPods, I warm up and begin to work through the series of exercises Mila outlined for me.

I'm more than halfway through my workout when my ribs start to protest. Sweat beads along my hairline and slides down my face, dripping off my chin, snaking down my neck, and wetting the front of my tank top.

My arms tremble as I rack the dumbbells after my last set. Hunching forward, I drop my hands to my knees and drag in a lungful of air.

When I stand, I cross my hands behind my head and my eyes snag on a familiar face in the mirror.

Cohen.

His eyes narrow when he sees me. He's talking to a teammate but wraps up the conversation and strides in my direction.

"Hey," he says as he approaches.

He's wearing a pair of shorts and a cut off T-shirt. His curly, light brown hair is hidden under a baseball cap and he's sporting several days of stubble that shouldn't look so damn attractive.

I remember Cohen from when he had a baby face. The man staring me down with concern flaring in his green eyes is nothing like the boy I remember. Now, he's all man.

I frown. Was I really so distraught over Brooks that I didn't appreciate Cohen's hotness when he stopped by my house a few weeks ago? How did I not notice...*this*?

"Rai."

I shake my head, and try to clear my thoughts, try to ignore my surprise over checking Cohen out. "Hi," I manage, bending over to pick up my water bottle. I grab a towel and sling it around my neck.

"You rehabbing here?" he asks the obvious.

"Yep. Avery cleared it."

Cohen nods, his hands resting on his hips. "You're pushing pretty hard. It's only been a few weeks."

"Nearly six weeks since my injury. I gotta get it back," I retort.

He nods but his lips thin. "You need a spotter?"

I grin and shake my head. "Nah, I'm straight, Cohen."

"Okay. Well, if you need anything…"

"I'll ask someone," I agree.

Grabbing my towel, I pull it from around my neck and snap it against his hip.

A few guys working out nearby chuckle and Cohen shakes his head.

"You're still a pain in the ass," he tells me.

I laugh and tap my butt cheek. "Kiss my ass," I toss back, sauntering toward a leg machine.

But I feel Cohen's eyes linger on my back and for some reason, it causes me to stand straighter.

I'm aware of his presence, of his attention, in a way I never was before.

It's irksome and annoying.

And yet, I like knowing his eyes are on me.

THREE
COHEN

HAVING Raia in the gym each day is distracting as hell.

The Coyotes facilities are where I come to check out. To turn off my mind and focus on football. On the career that has driven every decision—romantic and otherwise—that I've made for the past decade.

Now, Raia Callaway is in my space and every part of my body knows it. At first, I think I'm in tune to her because of our history. But when she starts a set of Romanian deadlifts, and I get a good look at her ass in her hug-every-curve leggings, I want to bleach my eyes, toss her a hoodie, and hustle her out of the gym.

Because if I'm distracted by Raia, every guy in here must be low-key fascinated. And that bothers me.

Turning away from her ass, I throw myself into a workout. A DJ friend of mine sent a new playlist that I listen to—loudly —to drown out my thoughts. Still, I'm aware of every move Raia makes from the corner of my eye. And when she squirts a stream of water into her mouth and a few droplets drip down the column of her neck and fucking Gutierrez approaches her, my workout is effectively over.

"You're looking good, G," Raia tells him as I pull out my AirPod.

I frown. Gutierrez looks like a sweaty, smelly dumpster.

"Thanks. The rehab's been a bitch," Gage replies.

"Tell me about it." She points to the side of her body. "But my injury is nothing compared to yours. You starting this season?"

"God, I hope so," he replies, leaning against a Smith machine.

Raia sighs. "I hope so, too."

Gage casually taps her arm. "You'll get back out there. Don't give up on what you want, Raia. And definitely not for a man."

She winces. "You heard, huh?"

"Brooks always was a chump," he admits and Raia's shoulders dip.

Is she embarrassed or relieved by Gage's assessment? And why can't I tell? I used to read Raia's mood by the most subtle lift of her eyebrow, by a twist in her lips, and now...*I don't know.*

That bothers me too.

I saunter over to interrupt their conversation.

"What are you slackers doing?" I ask.

Gage snorts and slaps my shoulder. "Slackers? I saw you dancing more than you were lifting, Cohen."

I tap to the AirPod still in my ear. "Skillet sent me a new playlist."

"Dope. AirDrop it to me?" Gage asks. "I could use the extra motivation."

"No doubt," I agree, pulling out my phone to drop him the playlist. I arch an eyebrow at Raia.

"I'll take it, too," she says. No please. No gratitude.

I grin. Fuck, I missed this pain in the ass.

"Number?" I ask, even though I have it. I've had her digits since she first got a cell phone at age thirteen.

Surprise crosses her face, but she doesn't say anything. Instead, she rattles off the numbers and I pop them into my phone. Sure enough, Raia's name appears on the screen.

I send her the playlist.

"Thanks, man." Gage shakes his phone at me. "I gotta catch up with the rookie." He flips his chin toward West. "Good to see you, Rai."

"You too, G. Take it easy," Raia replies. She glances at me. Her cheeks are red from her workout, and she has a few strands of hair plastered to her neck with sweat. The front of her tank has a wet patch in the valley between her perky breasts and I quickly avert my gaze.

When did Raia become such a...woman? When the hell did she grow up?

"How'd it go today?" She looks like she pushed hard. Too hard? What is she trying to prove? While I've had a front-row seat to the competitive nature of the Callaway siblings for years, I've also witnessed both of them do physical damage when their mental motivation burns too bright.

"Fine," she replies, moving her arm to stretch out her shoulder. She blows out a sigh. "The injury isn't as bad as I feared. I'm not in as much pain as I thought I'd be."

"Wait 'til tomorrow."

Raia flips me the middle finger and I smack her hand away.

She grins. "How was your workout? Looked pretty light to me."

"So, you were watching me, then?" I toss back.

She blushes. Such a pretty pink.

Fuck, what the hell am I doing? Flirting with Raia? Raia!

"Nah," she recovers. "Just every time I finished a set, you were still standing in the same spot."

I chuckle. "I already worked out this morning. Ran too." I blow her a teasing kiss.

She groans. "You and my brother are the worst. What is

wrong with the two of you? Why do you always have to go at everything with one-hundred percent?"

I flex obnoxiously. "It's how champions are made, babe."

She lifts an eyebrow. Is it at my teasing tone? Or the term of endearment that just slipped out at the end? I hope she doesn't read into it. I call nameless women "babe" all the damn time.

But Raia's not nameless. She's working her way under my damn skin.

Her phone chirps in quick succession, interrupting our wordless stare-off.

She pulls her phone from the front of her small bag and shakes her head as she swipes to read the messages.

Her complexion pales and her eyes widen. Her lips part and a look of pure panic crosses her expression. Then, gut-wrenching heartache. Her shoulders slump and she sucks in an inhale that cracks like a sob.

"Raia?" I step toward her.

She reaches out, as if looking for a bench, or a wall, to lean her weight against. She sways on her feet, and I swear, taking her arm to pull her toward a seating cluster.

I push her down into a chair and watch her closely.

Her fingers tremble as she swipes the screen of her phone.

"Rai?" I keep my voice low. "Is everything okay? You look like you saw a ghost."

Raia ignores my attempt at levity and my concern surges. If she's not flipping me shit, then something is wrong. My eyes swing around the gym. and I clock Avery on a treadmill. So, it's not her brother.

"Your parents?" I press.

"They're fine," she answers automatically. Her eyes don't leave her phone's screen.

I perch on the edge of the small table in front of her and lean forward. My hand lands on her thigh, right above her knee, and a jolt—some type of awareness—flows through my veins.

What the hell is going on?

I give her a little shake. "Talk to me, Rai. You okay, babe? What's going on?"

She looks up from her phone and stares at me with big, heavy, gray eyes. Like thunderclouds desperate to pour some rain.

"Cohen," her voice catches.

"I'm right here. What happened?"

She shakes her head in disbelief. "I don't, I don't understand."

"Want me to get Avery?" I offer. Maybe this is a family issue, and she would feel more comfortable talking to her brother.

"No!" Her hand darts out and wraps around my wrist, anchoring my hold on her leg. "No, please. I just, I need to go. I can't be here right now."

She stands abruptly, releasing my hand and shaking off my touch. "My water bottle and bag..." she murmurs to herself, glancing around for her belongings.

"Just, sit tight," I say, standing. I gently push her back into the chair and scurry to gather her stuff.

When I appear at her side and press her bag into her hands, the gratitude that shimmers in her tear-filled eyes makes my chest ache.

"Come on." I tug her up and wrap my arm around her shoulders. "Let's get you home."

She shudders before melting into my side. My worry skyrockets that she allows me to guide her out of the gym and into the parking lot.

Raia Callaway hates to show weakness. Or worse, vulnerability. She's tough, edgy, and likes to prove herself. The fact that she's letting me lead right now means she's truly rattled. And I fucking hate it. My protective instincts flare as Raia, small and fragile in this moment, clings to me.

Did someone hurt her? Is someone threatening her? What the fuck happened to make her demeanor flip?

She sniffles as we near my SUV and horror fills me.

"Are you crying?" I ask, the question popping out from my surprise.

She drops her head and I feel worse.

"You can cry all you want, champ," I mutter, pulling her close and kissing the top of her head. "I just, fuck, Rai..." I pause beside my SUV and pull back to look at her. "Tell me what's going on."

She stares at me with pure heartbreak in her eyes. Her lips part and her mouth forms words but no sound comes out.

"Jesus," I mutter, bundling her into the passenger seat of my SUV. I slide behind the wheel.

"My car's in the lot." She points a few rows over.

I shrug. "I'll get it for you later. I'm not letting you drive when you can barely form sentences." I don't mean to sound insensitive, but I'm worried about her. She's not giving me any insight into what has her spooked.

Raia runs her thumb over her leggings, scratching at the fabric. "Thanks for the ride, Cohen."

"Anything for you, Rai. You know that." I glance at her as I pull out of the lot. "What's going on?"

She blinks rapidly, holding back tears. "Brooks has a new girlfriend."

I fight the urge to slam on the breaks.

This is about fucking Brooks?

We just bolted from the gym—ditching my workout and leaving most of my shit and her car behind—because Brooks is *dating*?

Does she really care this much?

Raia sniffles again and I glance skyward, searching for patience since she's clearly devastated by this news.

I bite back every swear word filtering through my mind and exhale. I got this. I can do girl talk. Hell knows I've done it with Mila and Maisy on too many occasions. "Well, you knew this would happen eventually. And I'm sure this girl is random. I doubt he even likes her—he's probably just using her to get over you because—"

"It's Anna," Raia sobs.

This time, I do slam on the breaks. My arm shoots out to serve as a shield for Raia's body as my sudden stop propels her forward. Her chest bounces off my arm before she sits back in her seat and looks at me.

"Anna? Your cousin Anna?" I confirm.

Raia's tear-stained, miserable face meets mine. She nods.

"Shit," I swear, understanding why Raia is so upset.

Her ex-boyfriend and her cousin betrayed her on a whole new level.

They broke her fucking heart.

FAYE

Can you pick up your phone?

I can't believe she posted that photo without talking to you! If I'd known, I would have called you asap. I was giving Anna the chance to do the right thing, which she obviously didn't.

I'm sorry, Raia. Are you okay? How are you handling this?

ANNA

Raia, please, talk to me. I never wanted to hurt you. It just…it happened. Brooks and I wanted to tell you together. We were going to talk to you this weekend…

BECKETT

Fuck, girl, I get why you're off the grid but do me a solid and send proof of it?

BROOKS

Raia, we should talk.

BECKETT

Rai, it's been two weeks. You can't wallow for the entire month of September...

FAYE

Raia, please return my phone calls. I'm worried about you.

PRESTON

I could murder Brooks for fucking this up so badly, but you are not allowed—NOT ALLOWED—to bail on our ski weekend, Raia Callaway.

Brooks never deserved you anyway.

You're my ski buddy. You know I got your back, right?

FAYE

Hello? Don't make me call your brother... because I will.

ANNA

Your parents are coming for dinner on Sunday. Will you come too? Please. It will give us a chance to talk...

BECKETT

I got you a new sticker for your ski helmet.

(image of a phoenix)

Get it? Rising from the ashes. That's you, dude!

COHEN

There's a buttermilk pie from Annabelle's and a latte on your doorstep.

I DROP my phone and pull my head out from underneath the pillow. I groan as the daylight streaming through the windows assaults my eyes.

Mom must have opened my blinds. Why? Doesn't she know I'm hiding from the world? Nursing a broken heart?

Right now, the only person who understands is Cohen because he keeps bringing me things I need.

Pies. Ice cream. Chocolate.

Not platitudes and half-sincere apologies.

The truth is, I know my brother and parents aren't upset that Brooks and I broke up. Deep down, I don't think they ever liked him. But for him to move on with Anna, my Anna, my family, is crushing.

How could she do this to me? Were they hooking up before Brooks broke it off? For how long? Did our friends— Faye, Beckett, and Preston—know? Did everyone plot behind my back?

And how could Anna announce it to the world — to me — through a social media post? Doesn't she care about me, about our friendship, enough to have a conversation first?

These thoughts circle in my mind on a loop, keeping me up at night and making fresh waves of tears spill from my eyes.

Brooks and Anna are dating.

Messages pour in from friends and acquaintances from boarding school and college, pretending to worry about my well-being when they're really thirsty for the tea. As my humiliation mounts, I know I need to shake off my hurt and focus on my training. On soccer.

But this time, I haven't been able to rise to the challenge. Instead, I've spent the past two weeks hiding, and hating myself for it. While my friends continue to call and message, I remain in my dark bedroom with protective pillows and the steady delivery of sweet treats from Cohen.

"Oh good, you're up!" Mom smiles.

I groan and flop back into my bed, pulling the pillow over my face.

"So fucking dramatic," my brother mutters from the doorway.

"Be nice," Mom admonishes. She pulls the pillow off my face. "But it is time to get up, Raia. We've let you wallow long enough."

"What's long enough?" I muse.

"It's been weeks. You smell. And you're fucking yourself over by not working out your shoulder and focusing on your career," Avery spells it out.

I close my eyes. As much as I want to lash out at Avery, deep down, I know I need some of his tough love right now.

"Come on, I'll run you through a workout," Avery offers.

I lift my head. Exercise is my brother's love language. If he's offering to lift with me, it means he's worried. For some reason, his concern makes me feel better. "Really?"

His expression softens. "Really." He lends me a hand. "We'll start with a run."

I take it and allow him to pull me up into a seated position. "I think there's a pie on—"

"I gave it to the neighbors," Avery says.

"What?" I gasp, crestfallen.

"Oh, don't listen to him." Mom swats at Avery. "You can have a slice after supper."

"You need to stop eating that shit," Avery says. "I told Cohen to knock it off. You can have the coffee." He passes me the latte. The label on the cup is the Coffee Grid and I smile. Cohen knows me so well. "Drink this. Then, we go for a run."

"You're a tyrant." I take a sip of the latte and close my eyes in appreciation. Right now, I need the caffeine hit.

"You need more than a tyrant to get you back in soccer shape," Avery claps back. "Let's go."

I wait for him and my mom to leave my room before dragging my body from bed. I change into a sports bra and leggings and ignore all the messages I received save for one.

RAIA

> Thanks for thinking of me. Avery's making me run before I'm allowed to have any pie...but the coffee is giving me life this morning.

I'm nearly out the door when my phone buzzes. Glancing at the screen, I smile.

COHEN

> I got you, champ.

Each day over the following week is marginally better. I manage to pull myself from bed, run with my brother, get in a workout, and shower.

It's hard to confide in any of my friends since they're all tangled up in the group. Brooks, Beckett, and Preston roomed across the hall from Faye, Anna, and me during our first year at Althorp Prep. We forged an important bond from the start and have been each other's confidants ever since.

When Brooks and I started dating, there was worry among the group that if we broke up, it would ruin our larger, collective friendships. Would we allow something like our relationship to break apart the group?

Hmm, what happens when another member of the group, the cousin and best friend for example, go behind the girl's back and fuck her man?

I wonder what everyone thinks now.

Gah, I'm bitter. And sad. And angry as hell.

The problem is, I have nowhere to channel it. I'm ignoring my friends. I don't know the full story and I'm not sure I want to know the details.

My usual outlet, soccer, is currently nonexistent.

A knock sounds on my bedroom door. Avery pops his head in my room. "You ready?"

I throw a pillow at his face.

He chuckles. "See you on the porch in five."

Groaning, I drag myself from bed, and meet Avery. We start down the street at an easy jog.

"Use the anger to fuel you," he comments after a stretch of silence.

I glance at him. "You reading my mind?"

"Nah, you look like you're about to have smoke coming out your ears."

"Fuck off," I swear, picking up the pace.

Avery matches me easily. "You're angry."

"I'm furious," I admit. "Anna…"

Avery gives me a quick look before turning back toward the street. We make a left and continue on the quieter road. "That was messed up. But you don't know the full story."

"I don't want to know the full story."

"Yet," Avery supplies. "Because you're angry." With that, he takes off, kicking dust up in his wake.

"Fuck," I swear again, pushing myself to catch him.

My heartbeat pounds in my temples, my feet slam against the pavement, and my arms swing.

Hurt and anger swirl in my veins, propelling me forward, making me run faster.

I catch Avery as we near a stop sign and he pauses.

I stop beside him, dropping my hands to my knees and dragging in a lungful of air.

"Caught you," I mutter.

"Yep," he agrees, a ribbon of pride in his tone. "Use the anger, Rai." He turns to face me, his expression filled with a sympathetic understanding that makes me want to cry. "I know it's shitty advice. It's probably immature. But I blew shit up between me and Mila. And part of me did it on purpose. When she moved on with Hardt, fuck, I was angry as hell. Angry with myself mostly. But I used that shit to show up for my team, to perform on the field, to lead the Coyotes. And eventually, I stopped being so goddamn angry and I started making amends for the shit I stirred and the hurt I caused. Anger may be a shitty emotion but it's motivating as hell. Use it."

I stare at Avery, heaving as I try to regulate my breathing. My brother is rarely forthcoming with his feelings. I know he regrets hurting Mila. When she started dating Devon, I knew it served Avery right.

But to hear him speak about his disappointment in himself and how his anger fueled him to become a better teammate, a better guy, well… "That's big of you to admit, Ave."

Avery snorts. "Growing up is hard, Rai. But we gotta do it eventually. I know it feels like your world is ending. I know you feel betrayed, and you should. But you outgrew Brooks a minute ago. Don't let his shit stunt you now."

I frown, letting his words sink in. Before I can respond, my brother taps my back.

"Come on, I'll race you to the Coffee Grid. Loser buys coffee." He takes off at a clip and I scram to catch up.

Avery is done with the sentimental chatter. Truthfully, I wasn't expecting the snippet he provided.

Avery is maturing. And it's time I do too. I need to handle this situation better. Be more honest. Especially with myself.

Thirty minutes later, after I purchase coffees, Avery and I walk back home. There's an easy understanding between us that reminds me of our childhood. Years ago, before I felt like we were in competition with each other. Back when we were just a sister and brother goofing around.

My phone dings and I pull it out. A notification from my social media alerts me to a new photo Anna posted. It's a picture of her and Brooks, with their arms around each other and their noses nearly touching.

My chest tightens, the back of my nose burns, and my knuckles turn white with how hard I'm gripping the phone.

Beside me, my brother lets out a low whistle.

"I'm not ready to be the bigger person," I admit, not caring how childish I sound.

"You don't have to be," my brother agrees. "Did you hear me at all? Use the anger."

At his words, the rage bubbling in my limbs expands, a red-hot flash followed by a cool, quiet, purple acceptance.

I didn't ruin the group; they did.

FIVE
COHEN

THE NOISE OF THE CROWD, clapping, whistling, and cheering, wraps around me. A shiver runs down my spine.

Man, that sound never grows old. It fills me with awe that this is my life. My career. I'm a professional football player for the Knoxville Coyotes. Part of the franchise that makes up the Pride and Joy of Southern Football.

And those fans out there? Some of them wear my number and have my name on their backs.

It's fucking surreal, that's what it is.

The first home game of the season never fails to fill me with a strange mixture of hope, gratitude, and a smidge of luck that I've carried since I was a kid.

My pop used to take me to this stadium, we would sit in those stands, and he would point out players to me. He would rattle off their stats like a mathematician and I would watch in awe, surrounded by the game we both love. Now, I get to walk out on that field and a piece of me owns it. The game, the crowd, the moment.

Beside me, Avery grabs his helmet. "You ready?"

"Ready," I say. I'm more than ready. Year after year, I put football before everything else—romantic relationships, family obligations, reunions with my college buddies. This game always comes first and today, I get to prove it.

We've won our first two games of the season but playing on our home field is different. The atmosphere is filled with more excitement. Energy buzzes through the locker room as we mentally prepare for the game—for our fans.

Avery's phone buzzes with a message and he snorts as he glances at the screen. "My sister's here."

"With your parents?"

"They're here too, but Raia's sitting with Mila and Maisy." Avery flips his phone to show me the image.

I snort at the picture. Raia's rocking one of Avery's old jerseys, Mila's wearing a Coyotes hat, and Maisy's brandishing a foam finger.

"Gang's back together," I mutter, half joking.

"Yeah," Avery agrees, chuckling.

But the words stick in my throat. Once upon a time, Mila and Maisy were two of my closest friends. Before Avery cheated on Mila and broke her heart, resulting in her and Maisy cutting ties with the Coyotes for the better part of a year, we were a unit. Now, Mila's with Devon and Maisy's with Axel, two NHL players for the Tennessee Thunderbolts. They're great guys and the girls are truly happy.

The fact that they showed up for us today, are sitting in our stands to watch Avery, me, and the rest of the team take the field causes a lump to form in my throat.

Shit. Why the hell am I getting so sentimental?

Is it because we're playing on our home field today?

Is it because I've missed my friends and the easy camaraderie we shared more than I realized?

Or is it because everyone—Avery, Mila, Maisy, some of my teammates—are moving forward with their lives while I'm stuck. In the same place with nothing to show for it.

No significant other, no family, save for my parents and

Cooper, to come home to after a long day, no tight-knit group of friends like the old days.

It's just me and football.

Another cheer sounds out and washes over me. But this time, the ring is a little duller. Emptier.

"Let's do this!" Avery slaps me on the back.

"Yeah," I agree, looking toward the field where my parents and Cooper are cheering me on.

Mila and Maisy and Raia are in the stands.

I want to make them proud. All of them. But I want to make myself proud too and it hits me…all these years of hard work, of discipline and dedication…it feels like I have nothing meaningful to show for it.

"Coyotes!" my teammate Leo cheers, racing past me.

I grip my helmet and jog onto the field with my teammates. Thousands of bodies, clad in crimson and gold, moving like a wave, dance around us.

It's exhilarating and incredible. It's larger-than-life and bigger than anything I've ever known.

And for the first time, I feel a twinge of loneliness.

My eyes scan the crowd and I spot my family. They drop to where Avery's pointing and I see Mila, Maisy, and Raia.

Our eyes meet. Hold. A flicker of recognition, of understanding, crosses her face and I try to smile but it slips.

She tilts her head, her grey eyes softening for a heartbeat. She gives me a gentle smile as bittersweet longing for old memories rock through me. Then, she straightens, points to the field, and lifts her eyebrows in a silent dare.

I snort, shutting out the nostalgia. Dipping my head, I nod in agreement. I know I have a job to do. Today, I will rise to the occasion and play my heart out.

But it's comforting to know that in a sea of thousands of people, Raia Callaway gets me. She understands that sometimes, you can be surrounded by noise and laughter, in the midst of living your dream, and simultaneously disconnected, and filled with loneliness.

It's the most terrifying truth I've ever experienced.

I blink and pull my attention to my team. To the field. To the game.

To what I do best: win.

The team comes together effortlessly. Partly, it's because of our training and leadership. Partly, it's because our core group on the offensive line has been playing together for years.

We can read each other's expressions and decipher grunts and snarls. We're in tune to changes in the air and vibrations in the space around us. We play the game of football like we're well-oiled parts of the same machine, working in tandem to achieve unparalleled results.

By the time the clock winds down during the fourth quarter, the Coyotes lead by three points. Still, when Avery calls the final play, excitement skits up my spine.

I love this game. I love the feel of the turf beneath my cleats. The rush of wind in my face. The smooth feel of the football when it sails into my hands.

I love the opportunity to push and prove myself. Over and over again.

When the snap takes place, I run down the field, gaining yards as I near the end zone. I dodge a cornerback, roll to my left, and look for the football. It's already arcing toward me, a perfect spiral.

I leap, catching the ball in my outstretched hands. Landing with a grunt, I cradle the ball and hold out a hand as I run the remaining yards into the end zone and score my first touchdown of the season, with my family, friends, and fans, cheering me on.

The crowd goes wild. Jag rushes me and smacks my helmet. Relief fills my veins, and my shoulders relax.

The past two months have felt differently, as if I'm on the brink of a transition. It's thrown me for a loop, as has Raia's presence in Knoxville.

But right now, I feel like my old self. I'm just a guy who loves a game so much, it lights me up from the inside out. I pull in an inhale and hold it in my lungs.

"Way to go, Campbell!" Leo hollers.

I point at him before flicking my gaze to the stands.

My eyes latch onto Raia's. She's jumping up and down, cheering loudly. She wrinkles her nose and blows me a playful kiss. My smile widens as I reach out, pretend to catch it, and put it in my pocket.

She rolls her eyes, laughing with Mila and Maisy.

I know they think I'm being a goofball, but I'm truly happy they're here. My past and present collide, and I know this season is going to be epic.

Talon Miller makes the extra point, and the crowd whoops with glee. Seconds later, the clock runs out and the Coyotes win.

Relief and pride surge through my veins as I rush Gage.

"Hell yeah!" Gutierrez smacks my helmet as our bodies collide.

I throw my arm around him, gripping his shoulder as I congratulate him. "You're back, baby!"

"We did it, Campbell," he replies, grinning broadly.

I nod, taking a second to appreciate our win before the team practically lands on top of me. We won our first home game of the season, setting the tone for everything to come.

With Gage back from a nasty injury, he tore his damn ACL in the first game two seasons ago, our new rookie looking to make moves, and Avery at the helm, the team is jiving. Everyone is in high spirits.

"We're celebrating!" Jag decides, doing some suave dance moves that kick up screams from a group of nearby women.

Avery shakes his head at Jag's antics but he's cheesing hard.

"Corks?" Leo asks.

"Hell yeah!" Jag agrees.

"You coming, Rookie?" Gage tosses an arm around West's neck. "You had a solid game. Two touchdowns!"

West clears his throat. "Thanks, man."

Damn, he's humble. He graduated in June from UCLA and now he's playing for the Coyotes, scoring two touchdowns during his first NFL home game.

In the handful of weeks I've known him, he keeps to himself, shows up on time, and puts in the work. It will be good to spend time with him. I don't think he has any friends in Tennessee, save for his new teammates.

"Let's do it," I say, heading toward the locker room.

The team goofs off for a few. Everyone is riding the natural high of securing a W on our home field with our fans cheering us on.

I shower quickly and slip a clean shirt over my head.

Are the girls coming to Corks? Will they hang for a bit?

My nostalgia returns, hitting me full on in the chest. When Avery and I first made the team, before Mila was hired as our PT, Mila and Maisy were at every home game and some of the away games too. Loads of nights ended at Corks or around the kitchen table at Mila's parents' house, eating cherry pie and playing cards.

Now, Mila and Maisy are in serious relationships with guys outside of our crew. Avery is in this weird transition between fucking every woman who flips him a smile and hating himself the following morning. And I'm…here.

Still playing the game I love but going through the motions of everything else. When did that happen?

I pause, my hand on the shelf of my locker.

Is going to Corks going to be easy, good times, that are reminiscent of the past? Or will the night leave me with a sour taste in my mouth, a longing for days long gone?

"See you at Corks." Gage taps my back as he passes on his way to the exit. "Come on, Rookie. I'll give you a lift!"

I swear softly. I can't *not* show my face, especially after our win. I'll roll through and if the vibe is chill, I'll hang.

If not, I'll bounce.

Happy with my decision, I pull my phone from the shelf and glance at the messages.

MOM

Great game, Cohen! So proud of you!

I grin. My mom is the best.

DAD

Congrats, number 82! See you at dinner this weekend.

COOPER

You're a fucking beast, bro. Nice game.

I scroll though messages from college buddies and old high school friends. My heart rate kicks up when Raia's name appears.

RAIA

Good game, Cohen. See you at Corks!

I chuckle. Little Raia Callaway is heading to Corks.

That's a new development since, back in the day, she was too young to hang with us at Corks. In fact, I barely remember ever drinking with Raia, save for a beer I would split with her from time to time so she wouldn't feel left out when Avery had friends over to chill.

I spritz some cologne and run a hand over my hair.

If Raia's going to Corks, I'll stick around.

I can't leave her on her own in case Avery slips out with his flavor of the night. She hasn't been home in a long time and things are different now.

A lot has changed in the years since I've last kicked it with Raia.

Namely, how curious I am about her. Intrigued. Fucking interested.

And that shit won't stand. Tonight, I need to shut it down.

SIX
RAIA

I SPIN on my barstool at Corks and take in the mayhem unfolding outside the closed-off portion where the Coyotes are celebrating their win.

Fans hang in clusters, staring at my brother and his teammates. Cameras are raised, snapping photos of everything and nothing.

The rookie, West, ordering a pint.

My brother scratching his nose.

Jag doing some weird dance moves in the corner.

I laugh. I can't believe people, particularly women, are so interested in this group of jokesters. Even if they are easy on the eyes and professional football players.

"So, how's it feel?" Mila bumps her shoulder against mine.

I stare at her and grin. "To be out with you guys now that I'm a big girl?"

Maisy laughs. "Exactly. Mar ai, I remember you begging me to let you use my ID. As every person in here didn't know you as Avery's little—un aged—sister."

I groan. "I know. It was s I just hated being left out, forced to go home with Mo d Dad and play freaking

Scrabble when you guys were all coming here for beers. It seemed so cool."

"And now?" Mila lifts an eyebrow.

"Not nearly as cool as I thought," I admit since it's just a bunch of people drinking beer in a bar.

Mila and Maisy laugh.

"But I'm happy to see you both. To hang again," I admit, biting my bottom lip. I've been home for a handful of months, but I still keep to myself.

Still, there was a time when Mila was a permanent fixture in my life. She was at my house all the time, there was a seat for her at the dinner table, and I was certain she'd end up my sister-in-law.

Then, I went to boarding school, her parents passed away, and my brother broke her heart.

Given the physical separation between us by then, it was a natural progression of emotional distance as well.

"I'm sorry, you know…" I trail off. Shrug. "I didn't keep in touch afterwards."

Maisy waves a hand. "Don't be. You were off living your life, the way you were supposed to."

Mila nods in agreement, her smile widening when her eyes fasten on someone behind me. "Exactly. And we're still here, living ours."

Her fiancé, Devon, steps beside her and drops a kiss to her mouth. His hand hooks around her waist and she looks up at him with stars in her eyes.

"Yeah, you are," Maisy mutters.

I snort.

"Devon, this is Raia, Avery's sister. Rai, this is my boyfriend—"

"Fiancé," Devon corrects.

Mila beams. "Fiancé, Devon."

Devon regards me coolly for a beat and I realize that

Avery's past with Mila would be worrisome. Or, at least, annoying as hell.

I grin. "It's great to meet you."

He doesn't return my smile and Mila's expression twists, worry in her eyes. Beside me, Maisy groans.

Then, Devon snaps his fingers and points at me. "You're Raia Callaway."

"Um, yeah," I confirm, confused. Mila just introduced me as Avery's sister.

Devon grins. "The soccer player! Girl, you should be in fucking Spain or something."

The tension leaves Mila's body as she understands Devon's hesitation. He was trying to place me.

I chuckle, delighted that this massively successful NHL player recognized me for my career ambitions. "I should be." I tap my side and give him a rundown of my injuries.

"Fuck," he swears and shakes his head. "That's rough. You'll get back out there." He cups my shoulder and gives it a little shake. "If it makes you feel better, you're an elite athlete. Only the ones at our level catalog our injuries like a fucking grocery list."

Mila rolls her eyes but dips her head toward me. "Unfortunately, that's accurate."

I snort.

Devon gestures to the three of us. "What are you drinking?"

"Margaritas," Maisy supplies.

"We'll take five," a big, burly guy with a deep voice says as he steps between Maisy's and my barstools.

"You came!" Maisy exclaims, pressing a kiss to his scruffy cheek.

"Wanted to make sure you and Mila had a ride home," the man replies gruffly.

"That's what Devon's for," Maisy says. "He's trying to live up to that fiancé status."

Devon snorts and flips Maisy the middle finger. She pretends to catch it and slips it into her pocket.

"Hi," the lumberjack-looking dude with the man-bun says to me. He holds out a hand. "I'm Axel Daire."

My smile widens. Man, this guy is big and growly. The exact opposite of Maisy Stratford and yet, I see them together. Maisy's relaxed and happy around him instead of tense and insecure, which I vaguely remember her being around her high school boyfriend.

I place my hand in his. "Raia Callaway. Nice to meet you."

Axel grunts. "Callaway? Avery's—"

"Sister," Maisy interjects. "But we like her," she whispers.

All of us laugh as a round of margaritas appear in front of us.

"To your season," I say, tipping my margarita toward Devon and then Axel. "It's awesome to have a formidable hockey team make big moves in Tennessee."

"We do like you," Devon decides.

We laugh again, tap our glasses, and take long pulls of our drinks.

"You're a fucking traitor," Cohen announces, stepping behind me and placing his big hands on my shoulders.

I tip my head back and give him a smirk.

"Good game, Cohen," Axel says easily.

"Want a pint?" Devon offers.

"Or a margarita?" Mila adds.

Glancing around the group, I realize Mila was telling the truth. Her complicated history with my brother is water under the bridge. She's truly moved on with Devon and, great guy that he is, he's accepted her connection to the Coyotes.

Still, there's an undercurrent of energy between the hockey players and the football guys. But everyone gets along fine.

Is this how things will be with my friends now? Will this

situation with Brooks and Anna be water under the bridge in a few years?

I shake my head to myself.

No. It can't be.

Mila didn't end up with…Cohen. My brother didn't cheat on her with Maisy. Instead, they both started relationships outside of the Coyotes circle.

I roll my lips together and realize how screwed I am.

I won't have the effortless friendship with my crew again. Anna is my family and was my best fucking friend. Her betrayal cuts through me and I down half the contents of my margarita.

From the corner of my eye, I note Maisy's questioning look.

Devon nods sympathetically and, assuming my injury is the root cause of my despair, tacks on an order of tequila shots.

Cohen's heavy hands squeeze my shoulders, but I don't turn around. I don't want to note the worry or worse, disappointment, in his gaze.

I just want to numb myself for a bit.

Because witnessing the ride-or-die friendship between Mila and Maisy and meeting their guys who look at them with pure adoration, makes me want to cry.

I'm truly happy for both of them. But I also feel bereft. It's as if a piece of me, one I took for granted and didn't fully appreciate, is missing.

Anna was my ride or die. Brooks used to adore me. Now, it's all gone.

The shots of tequila arrive and my fingers tremble as Mila silently passes me one.

We cheer and I toss the shot back. The liquid burns a path to my stomach, and I revel in it. Soon, my thoughts will slow. The hurt in my chest will dull. I'll be able to pull in a deep breath.

I wait for the numbness to kick in as I keep up a stream of chatter with Devon and Mila. Maisy pulls Axel toward the jukebox in the corner. Cohen's touch falls away as Gage drags him into a conversation with some female fans.

One of them, a gorgeous blonde, presses her impressive chest into his side as she asks him to sign her shirt.

Cohen jokes with her. Flirting is second nature to him, but he also has a serious side. He just keeps it under wraps.

The blonde touches his chest when she talks, and he dips closer so he can hear whatever she's saying.

A strange flare of jealousy licks low in my gut, and I turn away.

Cohen can talk to whomever he wants. I'm pretty sure my brother went home with a redhead ten minutes ago.

I turn back to the bar and signal that I'll take another round of tequila shots.

"You okay?" Mila's eyes, a startling blue, are shaded with concern.

"Yeah. Just been a rough few weeks," I admit.

Mila sighs. "Yeah." She glances over her shoulder where Devon has his phone pressed to his ear.

He gestures toward her, and she nods.

"Devon and I are heading out. But if you need a ride or—"

"I'll be fine," I cut her off, waving a hand. I smile at her. "Thanks for hanging today, Mimi. It was... I'm happy to see you so happy."

Emotion crosses her face as she pulls me into a hug. "This will pass, Rai. I know it feels crushing now, but it will get easier."

"Yeah," I agree even though I don't believe her.

"Call me anytime. I'm always here for you," she promises.

"Thank you." I squeeze her forearm. Even though I don't say it, things are different now. She's not Avery's girl but Devon's. Her life has moved in a new direction. If I'm being honest, a better direction.

"See you later," she says, moving toward her fiancé. Devon takes her hand and laces their fingers together.

I glance around the space for Maisy and Axel but don't see them.

Shrugging, I thank the bartender for the shot glasses.

Then, I line them up. Three in a row. And toss them all back.

Still, the numbness doesn't fucking come.

Instead, my phone beeps with a text.

PRESTON

> Stop ignoring us, Callaway. Pony up and answer your goddamn phone.

> You're coming on this ski trip whether you like it or not.

> Me and Beck will come grab your ass if you're gonna be difficult about it.

> But you can't break up the group.

> We need you.

> Fuck, I need you.

> Call me, Rai.

Tears prick the corners of my eyes as I read his stream of messages.

I need you too, Pres.

But I don't reply. I don't know what to say. I don't know who to trust.

"Hey, how many shots did you take?" Cohen reappears, looking alarmed. And blurry. Are there two of him?

I tilt my head to the side and stare at my brother's best friend.

"Raia," he says, grasping my thigh. "Did you take all three of those?" He gestures toward my line of empty shot glasses.

I trust Cohen.

The thought flickers through my mind and I smile. I have someone I can count on. Cohen Campbell.

Relief fills my veins.

Cohen stares at me with a strange expression on his face. I giggle.

"Fuck," he mutters, glancing around Corks. "Where's your brother?"

I shrug, not mentioning Avery's long gone. I slide from the barstool and clutch my phone. "I gotta go."

"Go? Go where?" Cohen asks, crowding me. He pins me between his hard body and the ledge of the bar.

Go where? That's a good question. I have nowhere to go. No friends to count on.

My phone buzzes again.

BECKETT

Do I need to come to Tennessee, Raia?

'Cause you know I will.

I frown. He will. Beckett doesn't make empty threats.

BECKETT

The ski trip is scheduled. It's the week before Thanksgiving. I need you to confirm you're coming or else… I'm coming for you.

I sigh. It's a half laugh, half sob.

"Raia." Cohen's hands are on my shoulders again. He's peering into my face, his green eyes vibrant. Worried.

Is he truly worried about me? Will a man ever worry

about me again, or am I broken now that Brooks chose Anna over me?

"What's going on?" He gives my shoulders a shake.

I roll my lips together as a lightbulb flickers on in my head. I have so many brilliant ideas when I drink tequila. I beam at Cohen. "Cohen."

"Yeah?"

"Do you ski?"

SEVEN
COHEN

"UH, WHAT?" I ask, trying to follow her thoughts. She's drunker than I thought.

"Do you ski?" Raia repeats as if it's a totally normal conversation starter after tossing back a series of tequila shots.

"Yes," I say slowly. "I mean, I know how but don't actively do it during the season because…"

She smacks her forehead. "Right. Football." She giggles again.

"What's happening right now?" I ask.

"I should go," she decides. She turns toward the bar to settle her tab and I wave to the bartender that I'll take care of it.

"I'll take you home." I sign for her bill.

"You don't have to do that." She points to the bill then at me. "You don't have to be nice to me because of Avery. I swear, I can get myself home. I'm fine. Better than fine actually because I'm numb." She laughs. "Finally. Fuck, Cohen, you know how long I've been trying to *not* feel?"

"Have a good night," the bartender, Saffron, gives me a sympathetic forehead wrinkle.

"Yeah," I mutter, knowing my night just got infinitely longer and more complicated than it was a few hours ago. But I'm worried about Raia.

Does she think I'm only looking out for her because of Avery? Doesn't she know how much she means to me? How much she's always meant to me?

And what's this shit about being numb? I fucking hate that for her.

No way in hell I'm dropping her at her parents' house to get the third degree when she's drunk and…sad.

"Come on, champ." I toss an arm around her shoulders as I steer her out of Corks.

I gesture to Gage and Jag that I'm heading home for the night.

When Raia stumbles, Gage gives me an understanding nod. There's no way any of us would leave a drunk Raia to fend for herself when Avery's not here to look after her.

But the truth is that I wouldn't let any of my teammates take her home. No guy but me.

I buckle Raia into my SUV and take the driver's seat. Flipping the ignition, I glance at her and sigh. "You want me to call Avery?"

She snorts. "And interrupt him and the woman he went home with?"

I wince. "You saw that."

"I did." She shakes her head. "I was so angry with Avery when he cheated on Mila. What he did to her was terrible. The way he handled things was all wrong. But a part of me understood it, you know?" She looks at me. Her eyes glint, nearly silver, in the dark. "They'd been together for years. They were all each other knew, had experienced. It's natural to wonder what else is out there, right?"

Slowly, I nod. Avery was one hundred percent in the wrong for what he did to Mila. He should have talked to her, hell, even broken up with her. But yeah, committing yourself to one person forever while you're in high school isn't for everyone. Raia's relationship with Brooks isn't that different than Avery's was with Mila. "So, you understand then, why Brooks—"

"No!" she cuts me off, shaking her head aggressively. "That's what I'm saying."

"What?" I scratch my cheek, confused. Raia isn't making any damn sense.

"I thought I understood. I thought Avery had a point, somewhere, but went about it the wrong way," she repeats.

"Okay…"

"But it was fucked up. You don't love someone, care about them, grow with them, and then fucking blindside them. It's a betrayal to everything you shared, all the things you promised. It's a slap in the fucking face and no one deserves to be treated that way. Definitely not Mila. And Cohen, not me either." Tears well in her eyes.

If Brooks was here right now, I'd deck him for making Raia cry. Then, I'd hit him again for making me navigate this shitstorm.

"I know you didn't, Rai," I say softly. "I'm sorry he hurt you, champ. But you're going to get back out there and—"

"I have to go skiing," she whines.

Huh? I frown at her.

She waves her phone at me.

I take it and glance at the screen, reading the stream of messages from her friends.

I feel her anguish. I remember how terrible the fallout between Mila and Avery was. How I lost pieces of my two closest friends overnight. How much it sucked to pick a side —I ended up on Avery's by default. The fact that we were teammates cut Mila out faster, even though I mourned the loss of her friendship and the change that occurred between Avery and me.

"Fuck," I mutter, dropping my head back against the headrest.

"Come with me," Raia whispers.

"What?" My neck snaps toward Raia.

She looks at me with big, pleading eyes. Her mouth is pinched at the corners and her hands are wrapped around my forearm, nails digging in.

"Pretend you like me," she continues.

"I do like you," I retort.

She shakes her head. "I need you to pretend to be my boyfriend, Cohen."

"Your boyfriend?" I sputter. My mind tries to catch up to her thought process but it's no use... She lost me. "Rai, you've been drinking and—"

"That's why I can say this to you. Be this...vulnerable." She wrinkles her nose in disgust. "I'm fully aware that I will hate myself, hate how fucking weak I am, tomorrow. But tonight, Cohen, please, my pride can't take another hit. Come with me on the ski trip. Pretend we're together. Let me save face in front of Anna and Brooks. And let me not break up the group." She shakes her head miserably. "I can't do it alone. I can't face them. I won't..." she trails off. "Seeing them together," she sighs heavily and swears softly. "It's going to destroy me, Cohen."

I blink at her. Speechless. No words fucking come.

Little Raia Callaway stares at me with those big, silvery moon eyes. Instead of tossing up a wall like I'd expect from her, she wears her heart on her sleeve. She's honest and desperate. And she...trusts me. The realization bowls me over because it's been years since Raia and I have hung out and yet, the history we shared counts. It matters.

There are things about her—like how hard it is for her to admit any kind of defeat—I understand better than most. There are aspects of my life—like my family, my drive—that she knows firsthand.

Most women can't compete with football. It's always been my top priority and as soon as they realize that, they bounce. It's why I'm hesitant to start something meaningful with a woman. It's why I never want to meet their families or hang out with their friends.

It's why I've never been on a ski trip with other couples or a friend group that isn't strictly mine.

But Raia doesn't have any expectations of me. She knows. This is fake. Pretend. Make-believe. It's an opportunity for me to help her save face. To step up for her the way I used to when she was a kid and some chump teased her.

Still… "Raia, the season started and—"

"You have a bye week. It's the week before Thanksgiving," she supplies.

I grin. I can't help it. "This is insane."

She nods and scratches at a spot on her jeans. "It is. I don't know what I was thinking. I just—"

"I didn't say no," I say slowly.

Raia looks up. She holds my eyes. Holds her breath.

"We need rules." I try to think through this in a logical, rational manner.

"Okay," she agrees.

"We tell Avery the truth," I start.

Raia makes a face.

I hold up my hand. "There's no way I'm going behind your brother's back. Besides, he's going to understand. He'll get why you want to save face in front of Anna. Trust me. I'll talk to him."

"Fine." She crosses her arms over her chest, her lower lip protruding slightly in a pout.

"You look seven," I tell her.

She flips me the middle finger and I laugh.

"What else?" she asks.

"Other than Avery, we sell it," I decide.

Raia's eyes widen. "You're serious?"

"If you're doing this to save face, then we need to go all in."

Raia looks skeptical. "What's in it for you?"

"Pardon?" I lean closer.

"I mean, I'm not really going to…have sex with you," she whispers the last part.

My face is on fucking fire. "I, yeah, no, I don't," I sputter.

"So, what's in it for you?" she repeats.

"Fuck, Rai. Who the hell have you been spending time with? Do you really think that's the only thing a man cares about? Getting his dick wet?"

She winces at my crudeness, but I don't care.

"Is this the shit your friends tell you? Beckett and Preston and whoever the hell else?" I argue. Placing a hand on my chest, I catch her eyes. "Do you really think that about me?"

"No," she answers instantly. Raia tucks her hair behind her ear and averts her gaze. "I'm sorry, Cohen. Really. I'm a mess right now. I just, I guess I don't understand why you would do this for me. I know I begged you, but really, you're not getting anything out of it. Not even—"

"Don't say sex!" I cut her off. That word, coming from her mouth, is pissing me off. "I'm doing it because I care about you, Raia. Is that so hard to believe? I've known you for forever. It's a favor between friends. We're definitely not going to cross any lines. Fuck, I'm not even going to kiss you."

Even though I want to.

I shake the thought away. *Focus on the conversation at hand.*

She tilts her head. "You might have to do that."

"Argh." I bang my head back against the headrest. This is already proving more difficult than I thought. But she's right. How can we sell ourselves as a couple if we don't even kiss?

How the fuck am I supposed to kiss Raia Callaway and pretend it's strictly platonic? That I don't feel anything more than friends?

EIGHT
RAIA

"THE SKI TRIP is eight weeks from now," I say, needing to take control of the situation since Cohen's frustration is skyrocketing.

Besides, now that he's agreed, I can't give him a reason to back out. As soon as Cohen said he'd help, I sobered up.

I can't afford to let this perfect—albeit dumb—solution slip away.

"So, we can pretend our budding romance started tonight?" I raise my eyebrows.

"Tonight?" Cohen repeats. "While you've been drinking?" His tone holds a bite. "Thanks, Raia. Let's let everyone think that I took advantage of you. What the hell?"

I shake my head, trying not to chuckle. Cohen really is a good guy. How Avery managed to keep him as a friend all these years is beyond me. "No, let everyone think you took care of me. Let me cry on your shoulder. Assured me that I'm not broken. That one day, I'll meet the right guy. And then, turns out that guy is you." I do jazz fingers.

Cohen frowns.

Shit. I sigh and open my mouth to add more unhelpful sentences to this conversation.

"Do you really think you're broken?" he asks, his voice quiet. His eyes are hard as they bore into mine, but his mouth is soft. Pursed thoughtfully. Wow, I've never noticed what a nice mouth Cohen has. Full lips, perfect teeth, a strong chin. My eyes travel lower, checking him out with abandon.

Maybe I am still drunk. I squirm in my seat, butterfly wings rampant along my rib cage. A shiver rolls down my spine.

"Hey," Cohen murmurs. He grips my chin gently and brings my eyes back to his.

I blink. *What were we talking about?*

"You're perfect, Raia. You're smart and ambitious, courageous as hell. You go after what you want, and you don't make excuses for yourself. You hold those around you to higher standards because you expect the same from yourself. You're smart and witty and fucking gorgeous. You're the whole package. So much so that everyone else appears chipped in your presence."

Oh. My.

That's what we were talking about.

My lips part as I try to suck in oxygen.

I think I just got high from Cohen's words. From the ferocious glint in his green eyes. From the pressure of his thumb on the center of my chin.

"You think I'm gorgeous?" I ask.

He smiles. "That's your takeaway from everything I said? You know you're gorgeous, champ. And your looks are the least spectacular thing about you. You're much more than you realize."

I pull in another inhale as my heart races. Cohen stares into my eyes, glances at my mouth, tightens his hold on my face.

"So are you, Cohen," I admit on an exhale.

One side of his mouth lifts in a smirk but he doesn't drop his hand.

A group of guys exit Corks and make their way toward Cohen's SUV.

"Your teammates are coming," I whisper.

Cohen's eyes flicker to Gage, Jag, and Leo before snapping back to mine.

"How serious were you about starting this…understanding tonight?" he murmurs.

I swipe my tongue along my dry lips and Cohen's eyes widen.

"One-hundred percent certain," I say.

The football players draw closer, their laughter wrapping around us.

"Fuck," Cohen mutters. His eyes track their movement again before meeting mine. "Close your eyes, Rai."

My eyelids flutter closed.

It's his only warning. In the next heartbeat, Cohen's mouth is on mine. His lips are just as soft as they look. His kiss is featherlight yet intoxicating.

He releases his hold on my chin and slides his hand across my cheek, cupping my face as his fingertips slip into my hair.

I part my lips and his tongue dips inside, gently dancing with mine.

Cohen kisses me like I'm a treasure. He treats me with care and affection and a sweetness I never would associate with my brother's charming, joking best friend.

My fingers curl in the hem of his shirt as I tug him closer. Jesus, I want Cohen to kiss me into tomorrow. To obliterate my thoughts. Fuck being numb, this, this all-consuming rush, is a million times better.

I want this. *Him.*

A bang ricochets through my head and I jump back, gasping. I clutch my chest as Gage's face comes into view in the driver's side window. He looks furious.

"Stay cool," Cohen murmurs, planting a steadying hand on my thigh as he rolls down his car window.

"What the fuck, bro?" Gage hollers.

Cohen shakes his head. "It's not what—"

"It's exactly what it looks like," Gage interrupts him.

Cohen grins. How is he so chill? "I was going to say it's not what you think. Me and Raia, we're together." Cohen glances at me to confirm it.

I lick my lips again, trying to get my thoughts together since his kiss scattered them. I place my hand on top of his and lace our fingers together.

Gage narrows his eyes.

I bite my bottom lip, feigning coy. "It's new," I admit. "But Cohen and I are figuring things out."

Gage swears. "Does Avery know?"

"Of course," Cohen answers smoothly.

Shit. Now we really have to tell my brother.

"It was one of Cohen's conditions before we started this," I add, giving Cohen a playful wink. "He wanted my brother's blessing…"

"Damn," Gage mutters. "You scared the hell out of me. I thought…damn, I don't know what I thought. Should've known you'd dot all your damn i's and t's or whatever the fuck the saying is."

"Dot your i's and cross your t's," I supply.

"Whatever," Gage says, waving a hand. He glances back at Jag and Leo. "You believe this shit?"

Leo grins. "Should've seen it coming."

"Should've seen what coming?" Cohen asks.

Jag gestures between us. "With your history? Not to mention your career choices—two competitive top-tier athletes—and you both hate letting others get too close? This was bound to happen eventually."

It was? The fact that Jag and Leo seem surprised yet not shocked is interesting. I never realized how much Cohen and I have in common.

"Let me get Raia home," Cohen says.

Jag snorts. "Yeah, like you're really taking her to her parents' house. Good one, man."

Cohen's jaw tightens and I squeeze his hand. "Good night, guys."

"Later, Rai." Leo waves. "Drive safe."

We watch as the guys pile into Jag's truck.

"Shit," Cohen sighs, leaning his head back. He rolls his neck and stares at me. "You okay?"

I roll my lips together, still tasting his kiss. "Yeah. I'm good."

"Okay. Come on, let me take you home."

I shake my head. "Take me to your place, Cohen."

"I, uh—what?" he stutters.

I grin. "When did you start sputtering so much?"

"Shut up."

"Let's keep our story going," I say, not wanting to go back to Mom and Dad's.

Cohen hesitates.

"Invite my brother for coffee tomorrow. We'll tell him first thing," I tack on, knowing we need to get Avery in on this ASAP, and hoping my plan convinces Cohen to take me back to his condo. I don't want this night, this moment, to end.

Not when I feel like I'm on firm footing for the first time in weeks.

"Fine," Cohen relents. "But you need to message your parents."

I wave a hand. "They think I'm with Mila."

Cohen grins. "I'm glad you and Mimi reconnected."

"Me too," I say, meaning it.

Even though Avery blew up the group, I'm glad we found our way back to each other. I wish things could be that simple with my friends.

I glance at Cohen as he pulls out of the parking lot.

While not simple, at least the ski trip will now be bearable.

I lift my arms above my head and yawn loudly as I enter Cohen's condo.

"Make yourself at home," he jokes as I collapse on the couch.

"Can I borrow a T-shirt to sleep in?" I mutter, resting my head on a throw pillow. "I can't believe you have decorative pillows that match your couch."

Cohen laughs. "That was Maisy."

"Figures." Maisy Stratford is all about homey, thoughtful touches.

"Come on, champ." Cohen saunters over, shoving his arms beneath me, and scooping me up.

"Wait! I can walk," I protest, planting a palm on his chest. His pec ripples and I gawk. "Hold up. Can you make your pecs dance?"

Cohen snorts out a laugh. "Be a good girl and go to bed, and maybe I'll show you."

I chuckle, sliding my hand along his muscular chest. "Promise?" My tone is coy. As much as I try to keep it light, I am definitely flirting with Cohen, which is dangerous, considering the favor I asked of him.

Cohen shakes his head and tosses me into the center of his bed. "You're a pain in the ass. Go to sleep." He moves to his dresser, grabs a T-shirt, and tosses it at me. "Bathroom's there." He points to a door. "Help yourself to whatever. And I'll see you in the morning."

"Huh?" I swing my legs to the side of the bed. My eyes dart around his bedroom. It's decorated simply, with dark furniture and cream accents. In fact, it looks like it could be in a model home.

Cohen tosses me a water bottle he grabbed from a mini fridge.

I roll my eyes. "Too lazy to walk to the kitchen?"

He grins. "I like convenience." He moves toward the bedroom door. "Night, Rai."

I tilt my head. "You're not going to sleep in here?"

Cohen lifts an eyebrow. "No way, champ. We already crossed one line tonight. Bed's all yours."

I snicker even though a weird sensation—like disappointment—rolls through me. I should feel relieved that Cohen's giving me his bed, not…let down. I shake my head. I must still be drunk.

It's totally the tequila.

"Yeah, well, you're lucky I kissed you back, Cohen Campbell," I call out, my tone teasing.

"Tell me about it." I think he mutters before the door closes with a soft snick.

Huh? My eyebrows furrow as I stare at the closed bedroom door.

Tell me about it. Did Cohen *want* to kiss me?

I snort at my thoughts and force myself to stand. Making my way to the bathroom, I roll off the strange sensations since Cohen kissed me and recall my good fortune that he's helping me out.

That's what I need to focus on. The plan.

So, no more tequila for me.

"Are you fucking kidding me?" A hungover Avery brandishes his finger at Cohen and me the following morning. "The two of you," he continues, gesturing between us, "are going to pretend that you're fucking—"

Cohen blanches and I wince.

"Just so you can save face in front of fucking Brooks?" Avery concludes.

"Yes," I state.

Cohen turns wide eyes in my direction.

My brother swears.

Standing, I make my way into Cohen's kitchen and pour Avery another cup of coffee. "Sit down," I tell Avery, placing the mug down with enough force to cause some coffee to slosh onto the table.

Avery takes the chair opposite Cohen and glares at his best friend.

"Remember when you cheated on Mila and broke her heart, caused her to lose her job, destroyed her reputation, and fucked up your entire friend group?" I ask.

This time, my brother blanches and Cohen swears.

Avery turns narrowed eyes on mine.

I grin and shrug cheerfully. "I don't want to ruin my friend group. I don't want to have some scandal. But I also don't want to watch Anna and Brooks make out and feel like I got stabbed in the chest repeatedly with a meat cleaver."

"Christ, that's graphic," Cohen mutters.

"I begged Cohen to help me. There's no one else I trust. Hell, Avery, there's no one else you trust. You know he won't take advantage of me or the situation. And you know I'll at least have a decent time on the trip instead of feeling uncomfortable," I continue.

My brother sighs heavily and glances at Cohen.

The two of them exchange a silent stare-off for several long moments.

Then, Avery knocks his knuckles against the table. "She's right. There isn't anyone else I'd trust."

"I don't want her to suffer any more than she already is," Cohen replies.

I stare between them, amused that they're talking about me like I'm not right here, orchestrating their conversation like a master conductor.

"But do you have to fake it in front of everyone?" Avery asks.

Cohen shrugs. "If one person, besides you, knows the

truth, how long do you think it will take to get back to Anna? She's your cousin, man. And if she knows Raia made the whole thing up, how will that look?"

"Pathetic," I supply for them. "I will look pathetic on top of desperate."

Avery nods, seeing my point. "Fine. I get it. I understand why you're doing it." He looks at Cohen. "Honestly, thank you. Whatever it takes to get my sister out of her bedroom and back to the land of the living is a win at this point."

Cohen grins. "Happy to help."

"I'm getting out of my bedroom," I protest.

Avery chuckles. "To run or work out."

"I went to Corks last night," I remind him.

"Yeah," Cohen murmurs, amused. "And look how that turned out?"

Avery narrows his eyes at Cohen and my heartbeat jumps.

Does Avery know? Can he sense that there's more happening here than I'm telling him?

"Oh, God, all we did is kiss, okay?" I announce.

Avery's mouth drops open and Cohen tips his head back.

"You kissed my sister?" Avery glares at Cohen.

"I made him," I supply. "Avery, I need this. And I need it to look real. I'm telling you out of courtesy and because it was one of Cohen's rules."

"What other rules does Cohen have?" Avery asks, his gaze still trained on Cohen.

"No sex," I supply, even though that was my rule.

Avery's face flushes and Cohen turns beet red. I fight back my laughter.

"We let the town think we're dating. We hang out, get coffee, go for a dinner or two, maybe hold hands and kiss once or twice. Then, we go on the ski trip, let my friends think I've moved on, and break up before the holidays. We realize we're better off as friends and it's amicable. Then, we celebrate Christmas, you guys win the Super Bowl, and I move to

Europe to play soccer. The end." I summarize the plan as I see it even though I've discussed none of it with Cohen.

To be honest, his distracting kiss, and insistence on my going to bed, ruined any chance of additional planning last night.

But now that I've laid it out, I see him nodding in agreement. My brother looks less skeptical of the situation as well.

"Sounds good, right?" I ask the guys.

"Sounds like a plan," Cohen agrees.

"It's not a terrible idea," Avery acquiesces.

"Great!" I grin, retreating to the kitchen to top up my coffee mug. When I reenter the dining area, Avery and Cohen are chatting about football and everything is back to normal.

I take a healthy swig of coffee and feel my shoulders relax.

The ski weekend crisis has been solved. I got this.

I can totally fake date Cohen without catching feelings.

I bet that kiss was a fluke anyway.

It didn't mean anything. None of this does.

NINE
COHEN

"YOU'RE MAKING A MISTAKE," my brother Cooper tells me as he adjusts his bike gears.

"It's a foolproof plan," I argue, wanting my brother's agreement. Hell, at this point, I need Cooper to tell me I'm not fucking up my friendship with Avery or my relationship with Raia by pretending to be her man for a few weeks.

"It's a disaster waiting to happen," Cooper shuts me down.

I sigh and turn away as I take a few steps toward his open garage door. Lacing my fingers together, I brace my hands behind my head and think this through.

A few days ago, when Raia laid out her plan for Avery and by extension, me, it made sense. It's simple and straightforward. We go on a few dates, let the town speculate, have a great ski weekend, and amicably break up before going our separate ways.

But...that kiss. I keep circling back to the way I felt pressing my mouth against hers, her soft skin under my fingertips, strands of her hair grazing my knuckles.

Kissing Raia Callaway changed things and I don't know

how to reconcile that with reality. I'm her fake boyfriend. Nothing else.

"Why are you doing this anyway?" Cooper asks. "I mean, I know you're going to do it regardless. You've already committed and now, you're backtracking, trying to get my blessing."

I glare at him. He grins and lifts an eyebrow.

"It's because I'm your older brother," he explains.

"Fuck," I snort. He's right. I always do things the way I want but at some point, I turn to Cooper. I want his understanding. I want to know that no matter what happens, he has my back.

And he always does.

"So, why'd you say yes? I know Raia's like a kid sister to you and you'd do anything for her, but agreeing to be her fake date seems kind of…counterintuitive? Incestuous?"

I swear as I try to form a better response.

Counterintuitive? One-hundred percent. I'm fucked up over a kiss with a woman I shouldn't be kissing in the first place.

Incestuous?

"What the hell, bro? She's not actually my sister," I blurt out defensively.

This time, Cooper is quiet. He watches me closely for several seconds before swearing and standing from the milk crate he plopped down on. "You fucking like her." His tone holds an accusatory note I can't deny. "Oh, fuck, Cohen. This is worse than I thought. Not only are you getting nothing out of this little arrangement—"

"I'm helping a friend. Someone I care about."

"But you're already conflicted about it because you *like* her."

"She's an awesome woman. Everyone likes her," I backpedal.

Cooper laughs. "It's not the same thing and you know it. She's your best friend's little sister!"

"I know!" I shout back, throwing out an arm. "Jesus, Coop, you think I don't know that?"

Cooper backs off and regards me carefully. "What changed?"

"I kissed her. Once. It was supposed to get the gossip circles going. It wasn't supposed to mean anything but…"

"But it changed everything," he supplies gently.

"Every fucking thing," I confirm. "And now, I'm supposed to casually date her, go on a ski trip, and then break up so we can carry on with our lives like this never happened. Like it means nothing. And you should've seen her laying it out for Avery, Coop. She's so direct and to the point. No feelings, no hang-ups, no mental agony over a kiss. It was just a goddamn kiss."

"Why'd you say yes?" Cooper asks again.

I shake my head and grip the back of my neck. "I can't ever say no to Raia. Never could, never will. But now, it's more complicated."

"I'll say."

"I need to help her save face, Cooper."

"Yeah," he agrees, dipping his head in understanding. "I just hope you don't lose yours in the process." He sighs and taps my arm. Giving me a searching look, he smirks. "I got your back, Cohen. Whatever you need. But brace for impact, brother, because this shit isn't going to be nearly as straight-forward as you think. It's gonna be messy and complicated. It's got little Raia Callaway stamped all over it."

I snort in agreement. "She always makes an entrance."

"That girl is larger than life. It's not a surprise a dick named Brooks couldn't keep up with her." Cooper tilts his head thoughtfully. "I think you could though. But you've gotta be all in, Cohen. Don't take this the wrong way but the only thing I've ever seen you fully commit to is football. And

Raia Callaway is an all-in or nothing kind of girl." He gestures toward the garage door, and we exit.

The sunlight assaults my eyes and I slip on a pair of aviator sunglasses as Cooper closes the garage door and locks up.

"Just remember…" He pauses a beat. "You have the power to hurt her just as much as she can crush you. Proceed cautiously," he warns before walking toward his car. "I'll see you at Mom and Dad's."

"Yeah," I agree, moving toward my ride and slipping into the driver's seat.

I pull out of my brother's driveway and follow him to our parents' house for our regular weekly dinner.

Cooper's right. I've never committed to anything other than football and Raia is an all or nothing kind of girl. But this is supposed to be fake!

Except it feels more legit than any relationship I've ever had.

Raia means more to me than any woman I've dated.

Nothing about this is simple or straightforward.

It's a disaster waiting to happen. And I'm at the center of the storm.

Cooper was also right about me moving forward with the commitment I made. It's a Campbell thing—we take our word seriously. So, even though I have concerns about Raia's plan, I'm still diving in headfirst.

That night, after a family dinner and hanging out at my parents', I text Raia.

COHEN

Hey, you busy?

RAIA

Ooh, my boyfriend! Never. I've been waiting for you to message all day.

COHEN

Cut the shit. Want to grab a drink?

RAIA

A drink?

COHEN

Yeah. Corks? Something casual...

RAIA

Well, since I already washed my hair...

COHEN

???

RAIA

You haven't dated much, have you?

COHEN

I've dated more than you realize, champ. And I mean that in the loosest sense possible...

RAIA

So, just fucked around then?

I wince at her use of the word *fucked*. I've never heard Raia use profanity until this recent trip home. But it makes sense; she is an adult now. She certainly looks and acts like a grown-up. A woman.

But part of me still remembers her with affection.

While another part of me wants her with a longing that feels both undeniable and wrong. Forbidden.

It's a head trip.

COHEN

Don't worry about it. That's not what we're doing.

RAIA

I know. We're playing house. Make-believe.

COHEN

If that's what you want to call it.

RAIA

How would you label it?

COHEN

Friends helping friends.

COHEN

You want to meet for a drink or not?

I need to shut this down. While bantering with Raia is amusing, it's also pointless. It doesn't further her objective and it confuses me.

RAIA

Sure. Pick me up?

COHEN

See you in fifteen.

RAIA

(lipstick emoji, fire emoji, dress emoji, shoe emoji)

"What the fuck?" I mutter, tossing down my phone.

I don't know what to make of Raia right now. She's still playful and funny, like always, but there's an undercurrent of flirtation.

Or am I reading into it because my feelings toward her are evolving?

Reaching into my closet, I pull out a pair of jeans and a knit, short-sleeve shirt. I need to pretend this is a date. I'm notorious for taking my dates to fancy restaurants to wine and dine them.

The fact that Raia and I are grabbing a drink at Corks will play into her favor. I'm mixing things up, doing something different. It will allow our neighbors to wonder if it's real. Given our history, I think most people will assume it is.

I just need to remember it's not. It's playing pretend.

Isn't that what Raia said?

I slip into my threads and fix my hair.

It can be as fake as she wants but I'm sure as hell going to look good doing it.

TEN
RAIA

GAH! Why the hell does Cohen have to look so damn delicious?

How can he make jeans and a shirt look this sexy? Especially for a drink at the neighborhood pub...

Rolling my eyes, I pull open the front door of my parents' house and smile.

"You're right on time," I greet him.

"I aim to please," he replies, dipping down to kiss my cheek.

His mouth lingers for a moment too long and I breathe in the scent of his cologne. Masculine, earthy, distinctly Cohen.

Why does he have to smell so good too?

"You ready to give everyone something to gossip about?" Cohen taunts, his tone low. Husky. Sexy.

I nearly shiver as his breath caresses my ear.

Nodding, I shuffle back a step and try to clear the fog from my mind. I smile brightly. "I'm ready."

"Good." He extends his hand and I take it, letting him lead me to his SUV and buckle me in. He gives my buckle a tug to make sure it's secure and I roll my lips together to keep from grinning. Cohen's always been protective and thoughtful.

He's going to make a special woman incredibly happy one day. The thought causes my smile to slip, and I avert my gaze from his.

Why am I thinking about Cohen with another woman? Right now, he's with me.

But it doesn't mean anything, my mind reminds me.

Another thought enters the chat: *But it could…*

Gah! I need to focus on the matter at hand. Faking it.

The driver's side door opens, and Cohen folds his long body inside, clipping in his seat belt and flipping the ignition.

"You good?" he asks, his tone teasing with all the things we're not saying.

We're going to play pretend. We're going to lie to everyone we know. We're going to fake date.

"Absolutely," I confirm. I need this more than Cohen realizes. His pretending to be interested in me is restoring the confidence Brooks bulldozed. His attentive concern is replenishing the betrayal Anna leveled me with. Cohen is doing more than helping me save face; he's reminding me that I'm not a failure. I can be a good girlfriend and a good friend.

I deserve better than what Brooks and Anna did.

"I told Cooper," he shares as he turns onto Main Street.

My eyes widen. "You did?"

"Yeah. You mad?"

"No." I shake my head. "That wouldn't be fair. I mean, we told my brother the truth."

"Yeah," Cohen chuckles. "But your brother is my best friend and teammate. I needed him to know so it doesn't affect our friendship or our team."

"Still, I trust Cooper," I say softly.

"So do I," Cohen agrees.

"What's he think?" I ask, wanting to know what an outsider thinks of our arrangement.

Cohen gives me a side glance. "He thinks we're a disaster waiting to happen."

I laugh. "Sounds about right." Especially with how complicated my feelings for Cohen are now that he kissed me...

"You don't think we can pull this off?" Cohen teases, looking at me again. His expression is open and playful. For a moment, he looks like the boy from my youth. "Come on, champ, don't you believe in us?"

"Of course, I do," I say enthusiastically. "It's just...I seem to cause chaos wherever I go. I don't want you to get caught up in my tailspin, and I'm sorry, because you probably will now that I've included you in this."

"Nah, you don't cause chaos, Rai. You create energy. And you didn't drag me into it kicking and screaming. I agreed."

"Thanks for that, by the way."

"Yeah," he says, reaching over and slapping his hand down on my thigh. "Anytime, Rai." He pulls into a parking spot and turns off his SUV. Glancing at me, he lifts a wry eyebrow. "Don't get too drunk."

"I'm never sloppy," I lie.

"I don't believe you."

I snort. "Hey! What kind of a relationship is this?"

Cohen chuckles and releases my seat belt. "An honest one."

Fair. I exit his SUV and meet him at the front. Standing straight and proud, I step toward the entrance of Corks. Before I take two strides, Cohen's at my side. He tucks me under his arm and holds me close.

I snuggle into him and we're a perfect fit. It feels natural.

Cohen holds the door open for me and I step in front of him, reaching back for his hand which he automatically slips into mine.

Maybe he knows I'm nervous. Or maybe he's just that good at fake dating. Whatever the reasons, Cohen and I enter

Corks like a couple. By the way patrons glance at us, no one doubts the truth of the lie we're selling.

I smile, Cohen chuckles, and we make our way to the bar for celebratory margaritas.

"Let the gossip begin," Cohen murmurs as he presses a kiss to my temple. He takes the barstool beside mine.

"I'll drink to that," I agree, pretending to ignore the cameras angled in our direction.

"How's it going?" Saffron greets us, placing down two coasters. She glances between us, and I know she's recalling the other night when Cohen settled my tab and escorted me home.

"It's going." I smile at her, and she gives me a knowing smirk.

"What'll you have?" she asks.

"Two margaritas." I hold up two fingers.

"And a bar pie. Margherita," Cohen tacks on.

Saffron nods and moves to make our drinks.

"Drinks *and* food," I whisper conspiratorially.

"I don't want the community to think I don't feed you," he replies.

"Right. You'd be labeled as cheap," I agree.

Cohen wrinkles his nose as if the idea truly offends him.

"Relax," I laugh, slapping his knee. "No one thinks that of you."

He places his hand over mine, keeping my fingers pressed against his hard thigh. "I hope not, champ. But just in case… I'll spoil you some."

"Only some?"

He shrugs. "Our expiration date isn't too far off. Gotta make it all believable."

"True," I acquiesce. "I like rubies best," I add, just in case he needs to know.

"I'll remember that," he replies, his eyes sparking.

"Here you go," Saffron says, setting down our drinks.

"Thanks," Cohen and I say in union.

Picking up my drink, I lift it in his direction. "To faking it," I whisper.

Cohen shakes his head. "To making it."

I bite my bottom lip to keep from laughing as we clink glasses. Then, I take a long pull of my delicious margarita and let the tequila settle me.

This is easier than I thought. In fact, this may be my best idea yet.

I'll drink to that too.

"Did you see his face?" I crack up as Cohen parks his SUV in front of my parents' house.

"He probably thinks your brother is going to kill me. But Cole's a good guy...and he's dating his teammate's sister so..." Cohen trails off.

I shake my head, recalling one of the Thunderbolts' hockey players horrified expression when he saw Cohen whisper nonsense into my ear.

But it didn't look like nonsense. It looked like something a man in lust would do.

"I think we pulled it off." I hold out my hand.

Instead of smacking it for a high five, Cohen grasps my fingers and places a quick kiss to the center of my palm. "I think we killed it," he agrees. "Come on, let me walk you to the door like a gentleman."

I roll my eyes since *Cohen* and *gentleman* aren't mutually exclusive in my mind. "You don't have to do that. It's just my parents."

"Are you telling them the truth?"

I shake my head as guilt ripples in my stomach. "Is it shitty if I say no? I know if my mom thinks we're actually dating, she'll pass that information along to Anna's mom.

This…situation…has put my family in a weird position. My parents are really close with Anna's parents. They don't want their daughter's relationship issues to come between them, but I also know my parents have my back. They don't like the shit Brooks pulled…" I sigh. "It's complicated."

"I know," Cohen says softly. "It's messed up."

"Yeah."

"But you want Mrs. C to buy that we're dating…" His eyes flick to the front door.

"You need to walk me to my door," I acquiesce before rolling my lips together to keep from giggling. "And kiss me good night."

I expect Cohen to chuckle. Instead, his eyes flash to mine. They're serious and intense. Deep and trusting. "I'm gonna kiss the hell out of you, champ." His words are playful and at odds with his low, husky tone.

My amusement fades as a shiver trembles through my body. Desire travels through my limbs, making me acutely aware of how incredibly good-looking and larger-than-life Cohen is.

"You ready?" he asks, his hand reaching for the lever on his SUV.

I nod, not trusting my voice. Not trusting myself at all.

Between the way Cohen's looking at me and the little sparks flaring to life inside my body and mind, I'm not sure about anything. A few hours ago, we were talking and joking at Corks. Now, I want him to simultaneously walk me to the door and kiss me senseless and sit here with me, sharing stories, until daybreak.

Cohen slips from the SUV and rounds the front before appearing at the passenger door. He tugs it open and reaches for me. Not my hand, but for *me*. His large hands grasp my hips as he lifts me down. My chest grazes his and I inhale sharply at the contact.

He places me on my feet but keeps his hands on my waist,

steadying me. I gaze up at him, noting the tension in his jaw, the tenderness in his expression.

"I had fun tonight, Rai," he murmurs.

"Me too."

Cohen laces our hands together as we walk, slowly, to the front porch.

He lingers on the bottom step, and I turn, tilting my head toward him. "Want to come in?"

A sly smirk plays along his mouth and his eyes sparkle. "More than I should."

My eyebrows dip. Am I reading into things? Does he want to…be with me?

"I, um," I stammer, searching for words. They all flee, and I'm left with nothing but nervous babbles.

Cohen smiles. He smiles and his face transforms and my ability to breathe stops. God, he's gorgeous. How is he still single?

I want to ask but clamp my lips shut.

Cohen's eyes stray to the window behind me before latching onto mine. He leans closer. "Your mom's spying on us."

I snort, closing my eyes for a heartbeat. "Of course, she is."

"How badly do you want her to believe this?" he asks, his eyes searching for confirmation.

My heart rate ticks up as nervous energy gathers in my hands. He's going to kiss me. And when he does, he's going to flip my world upside down.

I already know it and…God, I want it. Want him.

"Badly," I murmur, my voice laced with the lust thrumming through my veins.

Cohen's eyes darken and he nods, a sharp drop of his chin. Then, he palms my hip, slipping his hand to the small of my back. With his other hand, he tilts my chin.

Even though I'm standing on the step above his, he still has a few inches on me. His eyes flash to mine before dropping to my lips. When they meet mine again, I note the flicker of hesitation in his gaze.

Does he not want to kiss me?

Is he worried it will blur things?

Is my mom still snooping?

Before I can form a response to any of the questions in my mind, Cohen arcs his mouth over mine. Our lips crash together, and a reckless wildfire ignites low in my abdomen.

I moan, my hunger for him insatiable, as I move onto my tippy toes to deepen our kiss.

Cohen's fingers twist in the material of my shirt as he slips his tongue between my lips. It duels with mine, but I keep up, wanting everything he's giving and more.

Our kiss shocks my system and it's all I can think about, all I feel. In this moment, it's just Cohen and me. Our desperate hands, our greedy mouths, our heightening need.

The porch light flickers on and off several times and Cohen pulls away. Amusement twists his mouth, and his eyes are knowing as they flash back to the window.

"Mrs. C busted us," he explains.

"Ugh," I groan, mentally sparring with my mother. "She's the worst."

Cohen shakes his head and brushes his lips across my cheek. "Good night, Raia."

"Night, Cohen," I murmur, wishing I didn't live with my parents.

As hard as it is to walk away from the heat emanating from Cohen's frame, I force myself to turn away and move toward the front door.

It magically swings open before I can turn the handle and I snort. My mom is desperately waiting for details.

I give Cohen one final wave. He slips his hands into his pockets and drops off the steps.

"Call you tomorrow," he says.

"'Kay." I smile.

Then, I step inside and close the door, nearly jumping back as my mother looms before me.

"Jesus!" I scold her. "Did you enjoy the show?"

"I wish I had popcorn," she deadpans, fanning herself.

I laugh. "You're too much. I can't believe you flicked the porch light on and off!"

"You two were veering into inappropriate for the front porch behavior."

I roll my eyes. "I hardly doubt a good night kiss is inappropriate for the front porch. Besides, the neighbors should thank me. That was probably more action than any of them has gotten in ages."

"Oh!" Mom flicks her wrist at me. "Dennis from across the street has a new lady friend," she gossips, as if to one-up me.

"Good for him."

Mom grins. "Good for you!" She watches me for a moment. "You and Cohen, huh? I should have seen this coming…"

I pause my shuffle toward the staircase. That's the second time I've heard that. "What do you mean?"

Mom shrugs. "He's always looked out for you, and you always admired him… Now that you're both adults, it makes sense. And he's a much better fit for you than Brooks," she scoffs as she says his name.

Her assessment causes me to straighten and consider her words carefully. "You think so?"

"Seriously?" Mom raises an eyebrow. "Brooks bored you; you just didn't want to admit it. Now, Cohen…you'll never grow bored with him. He'll push you to chase your dreams too. Brooks neither supported nor denied you. He just…was there. Kind of indifferent to everything."

"Huh," I mutter, seeing her point now that she laid it out so plainly. "Why didn't you say something sooner?"

Mom smiles gently. "Because it's something you needed to learn on your own. And now"—her smile widens, and she gestures toward the porch—"you have. You and Cohen," she repeats, shaking her head. "You fit together. He's one of the best men I know," she adds, causing my stomach to tighten. "Oh, make sure you tell Avery."

"He already knows," I reply automatically.

"See?" Mom beams. "It's already a more mature, honest relationship than what you had with Brooks."

I wince at her use of the word *honest*.

"Good night, Rai." Mom presses a kiss to my temple before ascending the stairs. "I'm happy for you."

"Thanks, Mom," I reply, still standing in the foyer.

Mom's words rattle around my brain, sucking up the good vibes from Cohen's toe-curling kiss.

Cohen will push you to chase your dreams.

I think back on my relationship with Brooks. His frustration when I couldn't stay out late because of early morning practices, the way he shrugged when I told him about Spain, his breaking up with me moments before an important game. I never realized his lack of support, since he always technically showed up. He was present without being invested.

Brooks bored you.

Were we complacent? I certainly didn't have the same physical reaction to Brooks as the one Cohen inspired. Cohen made me weak in the knees. Simultaneously nervous and excited. There was an anticipatory thrill moments before his lips touched mine.

It was just a kiss and yet, it wasn't simple. Instead, it obliterated any kiss I shared with Brooks.

One of the best men. Mature and honest relationship.

I wince as a flicker of guilt licks in my abdomen.

None of it is real. But a part of me wishes it were.

Shit.

ELEVEN
COHEN

"KEEP UP, CHAMP!" I call over my shoulder as I blow past Raia.

"Ugh! You suck!" she hollers as I leave her in my dust.

Laughing, I pick up my pace, nearly in an all-out sprint. When I reach the end of the road, I slow down to a jog before stopping before the lake. I blow out a breath and tuck my hands behind my head as I regulate my breathing.

"Oof," I wheeze out as Raia hurls herself into my side, taking me out. "Shit!" I swear, wrapping my arms around her to keep her from taking the brunt of our combined fall.

Rolling onto my back, I stare up at the brunette beauty as she pins me. "I can more than keep up," she says. "I can over-take you." Her hands press my wrists into the ground as her chest heaves.

"Are you fucking serious?" I say, my frustration flaring.

Raia lifts her eyebrows, daring me. Challenging me.

"Raia! You could have hurt yourself," I remind her. "You're injured."

"I'm a badass," she corrects. Always so goddamn cocky and fuck if I don't love it.

Instead of giving her the satisfaction of knowing that, like always, she impresses me, I buck against her delicate grasp and sit half up, banding an arm around her back. "You're rehabbing an injury and tackling me *is not* part of rehab."

"I still could've beat you if you didn't cheat." She pouts.

Pouts! Like a little kid.

I smirk. "I didn't cheat. I tossed out another challenge."

Raia rolls her eyes. "You weren't supposed to sprint."

"You weren't supposed to try to take me out."

She giggles. Why the hell does her laughter sound like music? "Caught you off guard."

I scowl and tighten my hold. "Are you okay?"

Her smile widens. "More than okay, Cohen." Raia shifts slightly, grinding against me and I nearly see stars.

We're in a compromising position, yet I have no desire to push her away. Instead, I want to pull her closer. I want to flip her beneath me. Cover her body with mine, take her mouth, and do a different kind of sprint to the fucking finish line.

My palm spans the center of her back as my pinky finger drags along the edge of her sports bra.

Raia's pupils dilate, and she sucks in a breath. "Cohen." My name is a needy whisper on her lips. A seductive caress.

I groan. My name in that tone…it makes things that much harder. Pun intended.

I shift, trying to reposition her but of course, I end up dragging my hardening dick along her thigh. When Raia sighs, I know she knows that I'm hard as a rock for her.

Desperate and needy and sporting a boner in broad daylight like a novice. I'm no novice.

Instead of standing up, or feigning ignorance, or doing anything polite, Raia places her palm on the side of my neck. "So, it's not just me."

"What?" My eyes snap to hers.

"When you kissed me the other night…Cohen, you twisted me up." Her voice is low, her words measured. Her eyes are blown with lust and ringed with sincerity.

She was right; she's badass. Because I don't know many women who would own their truth the way she is. And it only makes me want her more.

"What about Brooks?" I ask, mentally swearing at myself. I need to put space between us, remind her that this is a favor between friends, that this can't happen for real.

Avery.

The Coyotes.

She's heartbroken.

I don't know how to do serious commitment.

The list of reasons loops in my mind.

"What about him?" she tosses back, a playful smirk dancing over her lips. She tilts her pelvis and I moan.

"We can't do this," I whisper, more for my ears than hers. My fingers slide up her back, underneath her sports bra.

"Yeah," she agrees, dragging her fingertips over my shoulders before dropping her arms at her sides. "I know."

Instead of releasing her, I tighten my hold.

"It's a bad idea," I continue.

"Terrible," she concurs, hooking her fingers in the hem of my shirt.

"It will complicate things."

"Make them messier."

Her eyes hold mine. Gray and bottomless. Fearless.

"Fuck," I whisper, my breath washing over her full lips as they part on a sigh. Then, I'm kissing her.

Devouring her.

Squeezing her ass and pressing her core against me.

She responds instantly. Her fingertips drag up my torso, her arms drape over my shoulders, and she threads her fingers through my hair. Her chest heaves against mine and her thighs tighten around my hips.

My hands explore the lines of her body, all delicious dips and delectable curves. As one hand travels up her side, my fingers brush along the edge of her sports bra, play over the sweaty material, and trace the line of cleavage I'm desperate to drag my tongue across.

Raia tightens her fingers in my hair, tugging gently. She rolls her hips once, grinding against me.

And I snap. How much control am I supposed to have?

I roll her over. Her ponytail swishes against the grass as she looks up at me, wide eyes and flushed cheeks. Fucking gorgeous.

Hovering over her, I drop my mouth to hers and press a series of kisses from her lips, to her chin, down the slope of her neck and over the tops of her perky breasts.

"I'm a sweaty mess," she protests, pushing my shoulder.

"I like you like this," I say as I flick my tongue over her sports bra, wetting until the outline of her nipple and areola are visible. She arches into my mouth. "So fucking sexy," I groan, reenacting my ministrations on her other breast.

"Cohen," she groans, sliding her fingers through my hair.

The sound of an approaching car causes me to freeze. I drop my head to her stomach and press a kiss in the spot above her belly button.

"I'm getting carried away," I explain.

"I like when you do that," she replies.

I shake my head and move off her. "We can't do this here, Raia. Fuck, I don't know if we should be doing this at all."

"I know," she agrees, pulling her knees up to her chest. "But when I'm with you…"

"What?" I ask, wanting to hear every thought in her head.

"I feel…like me again," she replies. "Does that make sense? I didn't even realize how much I was going through the motions until…until Brooks broke up with me and I came home. When I'm with you, I feel…lighter. Everything is more fun. Even me."

Her words gut me. "You've always been fun, champ."

"Yeah." She grins. "But with you, there's a freedom I

haven't felt in a long time. I know you won't judge me or make fun of me, and I can just be myself."

"Always be yourself, Raia. You're too special to tone it down," I reply, never wanting her to change.

"I want to do this with you, Cohen," she says, owning it and impressing the hell out of me. Again. "But I don't want either one of us to get hurt."

"Me neither. I'd never want to hurt you, even unintentionally." The thought alone scrapes at me.

"Same. So…" She tilts her head, studying me.

"So…" I plant a hand on her thigh. "You think we can keep things going and…have fun until the holidays?" I offer lamely. But I can't get into a real relationship with Raia. Not when she's moving to Europe. I can't do a long-distance relationship when my career is here, in Knoxville. Besides, I travel most of the season; we'd never see each other.

"Yeah," she agrees, her smile slipping slightly. "We can do that. But we have to be honest with each other. If it gets to be too much…we call it."

"Absolutely," I agree. A sliver of tension surrounding the plan eases since I know that for today, Raia is with me. But in the long run, I'm fucked, because she already ruined me.

"And this part"—she gestures between us—"we keep to ourselves. Avery doesn't need to know."

Guilt courses through me at the thought of lying to my best friend. But what am I supposed to tell him? I'm casually hooking up with your sister until we amicably part ways? "Fair. Before any of this, we were friends. We'll always be friends."

"Of course," she promises.

"Okay," I confirm. Then, I grab her hands and tug her up until she's standing beside me. Dipping down, I kiss her hard on the mouth. "Sealed with a kiss."

She snorts, a bubble of laughter erupting from her throat. "You're so lame," she informs me before taking off at a sprint.

"Raia!" I shout after her, confused by the change in her demeanor.

She glances back over her shoulder. "I'll beat you home, sucker!" she hollers before picking up her pace.

My mouth drops open in surprise for a full second before I scramble into a run. Raia's laughter trails behind her as I try to gain on her. But she has enough of a head start that she may actually beat me.

My little badass.

The seatbelt light flickers off as the plane reaches cruising altitude and I relax in my seat.

We're on our way to Phoenix and as tough as it was to say good-bye to Raia, I think the space will be good for us. Well, at least for me. I'm getting swept up in her and I need to focus on football. I need to regain some mental clarity.

"Dude, do you hear them at night?" Gage taunts the hell out of Avery from across the aisle.

Avery turns in his seat, his eyes flashing to mine before narrowing on Gage. "Why're you pressing my buttons? I don't even live at my parents' home."

Gage laughs. "I'm just saying…"

"It's weird how well you're taking this," Jag explains from Avery's other side. "I mean, this is Raia. Your sister."

"I know," Avery replies.

"And Cohen's your best friend," Jag reminds him.

I'm sitting in front of Gage, and I raise my hand. "I'm right here, fuckers." I lift my eyebrows at my teammates. "Why are you riding Avery's ass about me and Raia?"

Gage and Jag ignore me.

Avery huffs. "Yeah. Cohen respects my sister. He's known my family for forever and he's good to Raia. Besides, Raia's an adult. I can't tell her who to date."

"That never stopped you from weighing in on her life before," Gage shuts it down.

"Like that time you told her she couldn't pledge a sorority," Leo unhelpfully recalls from behind Avery.

"Or that she shouldn't go on vacation with Brooks," Gage adds.

"Or move in with him," Jag states.

I snort. "And he was right because their shit didn't last."

Gage leans into the aisle to look at me, a shit-eating grin spreading over his face. "How long, exactly, were you waiting in the wings to swoop in and claim little Raia Callaway?"

"Fuck off," I bite out. A twinge of guilt assaults my gut since I hate lying to my teammates, my friends. The guilt is accompanied by an array of conflicting feelings. Because while I haven't exactly been waiting in the wings, now that I've swept in and "claimed" Raia, I don't want to let her go either.

Gage and Jag crack up.

Avery scoffs and replaces his AirPod, pressing play on whatever playlist he's listening to.

I turn away and close my eyes, hoping to sleep for the remainder of the flight. This week's practices have been brutal and the game against Phoenix promises to be tough. Plus, next week we play in Atlanta.

Fortunately, sleep claims me and I pass out until the plane lands. The team rides to the hotel together and my teammates check into their rooms.

"We're all on the seventh floor," Avery says, tapping his key card for the hotel room beside mine.

"Cool," I say, hitching my duffle bag higher on my shoulder.

"You hungry?" Avery asks as his door swings open. He grasps the handle of his suitcase.

I shrug. "Sure. Let me change and we'll grab a bite."

"Sounds good. These next few weeks are going to be intense."

"Tell me about it," I agree, mentally flipping through the games on our schedule. "It's lucky the week of Raia's ski trip is our bye week."

"Yeah," Avery chuckles. "You know, you're taking the ribbing pretty good." He gestures down the hallway, indicating the hotel rooms claimed by our teammates.

"So are you."

"Yeah, because I know you're helping my sister out. But the boys have been going at you pretty hard."

I shrug. "It's fine. Letting it roll off my back."

Avery makes a noncommittal sound in the back of his throat. "I'm just saying, I appreciate it. What you're doing for Raia, looking out for her, it's cool of you, Cohen."

"Of course," I say, my stomach souring. "It's Raia, I'll always show up for her."

"I know," Avery replies. "Meet you back here in ten?"

"Okay," I agree, entering my hotel room and pulling my suitcase behind me.

My phone dings and I check the message. I can't help the smile that forms when I read Raia's name, or the groan that slips out when I click on the picture she sent.

It's an image of her. Her lips her pursed in a kiss; her grey eyes filled with laughter. She's wearing a lacy black bra, her breasts nearly spilling out of the cups. Her stomach is taut and smooth and, "fuck."

As I mutter the word, images of Raia straddling me, slipping her bra strap off her shoulder, pressing a kiss to the center of my chest, filter through my mind.

While we've gone on a few more dates and fooled around some, we haven't had sex. It's as if we both know that once we cross that line, we're blurring every fucking thing. The truth is, I don't know if I can come back from that. One more step with Raia, and I won't recover. How the hell am I going to spend a stretch of one-on-one time with her at a ski resort, share a bedroom, and then walk away like none of it mattered?

It's a massive mistake considering our history. Considering my new, heady feelings. Our relationship has an expiration date.

Plus, there's my friendship with Avery to think about.

He's thanking me for looking out for his sister and I'm flat-out lying to him.

I feel shitty and unsettled.

Even though I know outing Raia would feel infinitely worse.

My thumb brushes over her sexy photo and I shake my head, pocketing my phone without replying.

The conflicting emotions battle in my mind as I meet Avery in the hallway, and we agree to eat at a taco joint we like.

For years, Avery has been my best friend and I've always had his back. Even when I didn't want to, like when his relationship with Mila imploded.

But right now, I'll do anything to protect his baby sister. Even lie to him. And fool myself.

TWELVE
RAIA

THE WEEKS LEADING up to the ski trip are busy. Cohen's football schedule is intense, and I attend every home game, rocking his jersey, and cheering for him in the stands. When he's not training or traveling, I'm at his place, spending nights cooking dinner together, watching movies, or letting him help with my workouts.

As my body heals and my strength improves, I start training with a local soccer team, ensuring that my time with Cohen is trickier to navigate.

While my brother's friends and teammates flip me shit, Avery has been surprisingly supportive of my whirlwind romance with his best friend. But that's because he thinks it's fake.

At first, I thought so too. But now...

As the weeks bleed into each other, that couldn't be further from the truth. My feelings for Cohen grow more complicated by the day. My desire for him climbs higher by the hour.

Still, he's careful to shut things down between us before we take the step we can't come back from. Sex. We both know it will lock us into something bigger, a more serious discussion and commitment. But I can't think about pursuing more now. I need to prepare to face off against my dickhead ex and backstabbing cousin. I need to prove to Anna, Brooks, and my friends that I've moved on. In fact, I'm thriving.

Hell, some days, I think I am. Each day spent goofing off with Cohen pushes Anna's betrayal further from my mind. Each night spent wrapped up in Cohen's embrace shows how my physical attraction to Brooks paled in comparison. It's a reminder that time spent crying over Brooks was a waste. While my feelings are hurt, it's obvious that I'm better off as Cohen's fake girlfriend than Brooks's real one.

As the ski trip nears, a part of me is looking forward to seeing my friends and spending time with the group, especially since it will mean stretches of uninterrupted time with Cohen Campbell, my not-so-fake boyfriend.

The morning of our trip promises blue skis, an on-time flight, and hours of conversation.

"Damn, how long did you pack for?" Avery asks as he pulls my suitcase from the back of his truck and sets it by my side.

Around us, travelers bustle, saying goodbye to loved ones or rushing to catch their flights.

I shrug. "I'm prepared for anything. All the things."

Cohen snickers and reaches into the truck for his luggage.

Avery narrows his eyes. "I don't want to know what all the things are."

I arch an eyebrow at Cohen. "There's a hot tub."

"Of course, there is," Cohen replies easily.

Avery pretends to gag. For a beat, his eyes dart between Cohen and me and a confused expression twists his features. But then he shakes his head. "You know, Mom and Dad, especially Mom, are over the moon about this." He gestures between Cohen and me.

"Yeah," I say slowly. Mom has gushed to her friends on more than one occasion about my budding relationship with

Cohen. A pit forms in my stomach as I look at my brother. Right now, I'm lying to everyone I care about. Friends and family. "I never expected Mom to be thrilled about this..." I bite my bottom lip. "Look, I know lying is wrong, and I feel bad lying to Mom. I feel shitty that I've been so focused on proving something to Anna and Brooks that I can't confide everything in Mom. But I need to see this through, Ave."

Reaching out, Avery pulls me into a hug and cradles my head against his chest. "I get it, Rai. I hate lying to Mom, too. But seeing you smile again and come out of the vampire cave you barricaded yourself in this summer, makes it worth it."

I snort and swat at him.

He grins. "Have a good trip. Show Brooks what the fuck he gave away. And let Anna realize that whatever she has with him, it still isn't what you'll have one day."

I nod, not trusting my voice.

While Avery's words are sweet and thoughtful, it's the *one day* that thuds in my temples.

One day. But not today. Because Cohen isn't really my boyfriend or my future. He's a ruse and now, I don't want to give him up.

"We better get going," Cohen says, clearing his throat.

"Right," I agree. I pull back and press a kiss to Avery's cheek. "Enjoy your week off. What are you getting into?"

Avery shrugs, another unreadable look crossing his face. "You know, a little of this, a little of that."

"Cryptic as fuck, bro," Cohen comments, giving my brother a look.

Avery shakes his head and jerks up the handle of my suitcase, pressing it into my hand. "Be safe."

"Thanks, Ave," I say, moving toward the sliding glass doors of the airport. "And thanks for the ride." Mom and Dad are already at work and saw me off this morning with pancakes and coffee.

"Later, dude," Cohen says, following me.

Avery slides back into his truck. "Call if you need me."

I grin and wave. It's strange but these weeks I've spent at home made me realize how grateful I am to have a big brother who watches out for me. "I will. See you soon."

Avery beeps once before pulling away from the curb.

Cohen glances at me. "Ready?"

I shimmy my shoulders and grin. "Let's do this."

We enter the airport and go through security. Once we board our flight and take off for Burlington, Vermont, Cohen and I both fall asleep. I wake up when the wheels touch down to find Cohen staring at me.

Clearing the sleep from my eyes, I lift an eyebrow. "Did I snore?"

"And drool," he informs me, swiping his thumb along my bottom lip.

I snort and drag the back of my hand across the lower portion of my face. "Attractive," I joke.

"Always," Cohen replies.

My eyes flick up to his and my breath sticks in my throat. How does he know the right things to say? Is he always this charming? Then why hasn't he had a serious relationship? I make a mental note to ask him.

The plane begins to taxi and the seat belt signal dings off, breaking the spell spinning between Cohen and me.

He sits straighter and breaks our eye contact. As the plane's aisle fills with passengers taking down their stowed carry-ons, I breathe a shaky exhale.

Now that we're here, in Vermont, my nerves are making an appearance. But I got this. I'm fine because I have Cohen by my side. He's not going to let me fail. He's going to charm the pants off my friends and make them fall in love with his easy humor, sparkling green eyes, and genuine charisma.

I stand and reach to take my carry-on from Cohen's hand. He scoffs at me and turns, leading the way off the plane, taking my hand luggage with him.

We grab our suitcases from the baggage carousel and rent the only car available—a mini hatchback that Cohen can barely fold himself into.

I crack up watching him navigate how to stack our luggage and then, how to accommodate the steering wheel and click in his seat belt.

He gives me a look as I stand on the curb laughing. "Are you coming?"

"You want me to drive?" I offer, giving him a cheeky grin.

"Get in the car, champ."

I acquiesce and ride shotgun. Punching in the address to the ski resort, I breathe a sigh of relief. "It's only an hour."

"Only," he scoffs.

I press play on the playlist I curated for this drive. As throwback tunes fill the speakers, Cohen relaxes, and my nerves ratchet up.

I pick at the cuticle of my thumb as my knee begins to bounce up and down.

I've barely spoken to Faye, Preston, and Beckett since Brooks and I broke up. I haven't exchanged any words with Brooks and Anna.

Are they happy? Still in the honeymoon phase?

Do they double date with Preston and whatever girl he's currently dating?

Did my aunt and uncle welcome Brooks with open arms or question how he bounced from one cousin to another in the space of a summer?

Cohen's palm runs along my thigh and squeezes gently.

I sigh and look at him.

"I can feel you thinking," he murmurs.

"Really? What am I thinking?"

"Things in shouty caps."

I sigh again. "Correct."

"You have nothing to worry about. We got this."

I start to pick at my nail polish. "I haven't spoken to Anna

or Brooks since… And I've barely talked to my other friends."
I wrinkle my nose. "What if they don't really want me there?
What if they only invited me—"

"They never would have ridden your ass the way they did
to get you to commit if they didn't want you there," Cohen
cuts me off. "They would have asked once to be polite and
then let it drop. Not threatened to come and kidnap you."

I roll my lips together, seeing his point.

"What else?" he asks. "Hit me."

I raise my eyebrows.

"All your doubts, worries, whatever. Lay 'em out,
champ." Cohen does a "gimmie" gesture with his hand and I
chuckle.

"We'll have to share one bed," I say slowly.

He beams. "Finally!"

I laugh and swat his arm.

"I'm not sure I'll be able to keep up skiing and snow-
boarding. I'm healed but my endurance isn't what it was."

"So?" He shrugs, tossing a wink in my direction. "More
time for us in the hot tub. Besides, I can't ski anyway. I mean,
maybe an easy run or two but nothing serious."

"Your contract," I remember.

"My contract," he confirms.

"Why haven't you ever had a serious girlfriend?" I
blurt out.

Cohen's head whips toward mine and his eyebrows lift.
"Seriously?"

I nod, my throat dry. I really want to know the answer.

He snorts. "Been waiting for the right woman," he says
slowly. His eyes turn back to the road. "Football has always
been my top priority. A lot of the women I dated didn't like
coming in second place. And I get that. But I also know that
the right woman will make football feel like an easy second.
No one has yet and I don't want to settle for anything less."

Oh. My. I sit up straighter and roll his response around my

mind. It makes sense. I like that Cohen knows his worth and won't settle.

But how long did Brooks take second place to soccer? And how the hell didn't I realize it?

"Tell me about your friends," Cohen says, changing the subject.

Some of my nerves dissipate and I grin. "You'll love Faye. She's sassy and spunky and hilarious. I know she feels caught between Anna and me and has been doing her best to show up for both of us. Preston is smart as hell. He may look stoned half the time but he's actually a badass hacker. He's chill and doesn't give too much away, at least, not at first, so don't be alarmed if you can't get a read on him. And Beckett, well, Beck's like a puppy dog. He's all bark, no bite, and loyal as hell. He'll probably want to be your best friend."

Cohen nods and I can see him turning my words over in his mind, placing my friends in different mental boxes. "And Anna? Brooks?"

"You know Anna," I remind him.

"It's been years."

"Yeah," I say slowly. "To be honest, I don't know anymore. A few months ago, I thought I knew Anna, and Brooks, better than anyone. But I never saw this coming. I never thought either one of them would…"

Cohen's hand on my thigh flexes. "Yeah."

We're quiet for a few minutes. The song changes and I drop my head back against the headrest, glance out the window at the passing scenery. As we climb into higher altitudes, the brightly colored leaves of autumn give way to snowy passes. The passing scenery rolls into winter and it's beautiful. Breathtaking.

I pull in a deep breath and try to settle the knots in my stomach.

"Hey," Cohen says, giving my leg a shake.

I turn to look at him.

"We got this," he reminds me, a promise in his tone. "I got you."

"I know."

"You want to make up a signal or something?"

"A what?"

"A gesture, something, for when one of us needs a save," he explains. "It will work both ways and be something only the two of us understands."

"Like...a safe word?"

"Jesus," Cohen grumbles, adjusting himself in his confined space. "Get your head out of the gutter and into the game, champ."

I chuckle. "What's our safe word, Cohen?"

"I thought we'd do a bird call," he offers, amusement in his voice.

"A bird call?" I burst out laughing and practice squawking.

"Oh, God, no!" He shuts me down. "You have to be more subtle. Like this." Cohen makes a throaty, croaking sound.

"What the fuck was that?"

"A raven," he says defensively.

"Let's be seagulls," I suggest, doing my best impersonation.

Cohen cracks up. He squeezes my thigh again. A little higher this time. "Christ, at this point, we can just roar like lions," he mutters.

In unison, we let out guttural roars before dissolving into laughter. We're howling—Cohen is dashing a tear from his eye and I'm clutching my stomach—as we take the exit toward the ski resort.

As our laughter dies down and we pull into the resort, I grin at my guy. "Thank you, Cohen. Truly, I couldn't do this without you."

"Yeah, you could," he refutes, removing his hand from my

leg. I immediately sense the loss. "But I'm happy to do it with you."

Swoon! Again, how does he always know the perfect thing to say?

I read off the directions as Cohen navigates toward the chalet our group rented. When we pull in front and park, he gives me a long, searching look.

"What?" I ask, my body already tightening at his heated gaze.

"Bird call or lion's roar?"

I chuckle, my nerves dissipating. "Surprise me."

"Always, champ."

Then, we exit the car, gather our luggage, and enter the ski chalet.

THIRTEEN
COHEN

THE SECOND RAIA sinks into her friend Faye's embrace,
I realize how much Anna and Brooks shacking up cost my
girl.

She misses her friends. These are her people and without
them, she's been fighting emotional anguish on top of physical pain.

As soon as Faye releases her, one of the guys—Beckett or
Preston—swoops in and picks her up, swinging her around
and whooping how happy he is to see her.

By her explanation in the car, my guess is Beckett.

"Get over here, Pres," the guys says, confirming my
hunch. "Our girl is here!"

Preston, clad in black sweats and a black backwards baseball hat, loops an arm around Raia's neck and pull her into
his chest. He murmurs words I can't hear, and she nods. He
pulls back, searches her face, gives a nod, and kisses the top
of her head before releasing her.

He's subdued while Beckett is thrilled. Faye, with bright
blue eyes and mermaid hair, joins in the scene with tears in
her eyes.

Again, it hits me how much Raia missed out on. This is

more than a group of friends; this is a family. Seeing their warm welcome unfold makes Anna's betrayal and Brooks being a dick land that much harder.

I remain in the foyer, clocking personality traits of Raia's friends and committing them to memory. This trip, I'm going to show every damn person in this house the way Raia deserves to be treated. I'm going to lay it on thick and let them all celebrate what a fucking upgrade I am over Brooks.

"Hey," Beckett says, extending a hand my way. "I'm Beck, it's good to meet you, man."

"Hey." I shake his hand. It's firm and I don't miss the curious glance in his eyes. "Cohen. Good to be here."

"Preston," the other dude says, giving me a once-over.

I tip my head in greeting.

"Hi!" Faye waves, walking over and giving me a hug. "I'm so happy you could make it."

I smile at her, realizing she's sincere. She wants to see Raia happy more than anything. "Same here. Thanks for having me."

"Of course," Faye says, wrapping an arm around Raia's waist. "This wouldn't be our annual ski trip without Raia." She leans forward and drops her voice. "Thanks for bringing our girl home."

I nod. Home. Their group, their family.

In a way, it reminds me of my bond with the Coyotes. The team spends so much time together, we witness each other at our best and worst, it's inevitable that our professional lives spill into our personal ones. But with Raia's crew, they're all friends because they chose each other. They stick together because they want to.

It's similar, but different than what I know. The only true friendships I've had are Avery and Mila and they nearly broke them. Raia has a whole tribe.

"Um, hey, Rai," a timid voice says.

Silence descends on the group. In fact, it seems like

everyone is holding their breaths. Slowly, my head swings toward the hallway where Anna stands. She's wearing an oversized hoodie I bet belongs to Brooks. The sleeves hang past her hands, and she curls her fingers around the cuffs nervously. Her eyes dart from Raia to me to Faye. Then, up to Brooks, who conveniently steps behind her.

His expression is unreadable. His hair is styled and he's wearing a Lacoste V-neck pull-over sweater over a button-down shirt. Always polished and presentable. It's one of the things that irks me about him. It's like he doesn't know how to be comfortable. To chill.

Sizing him up, I have no fucking clue what Raia ever saw in him. Sure, he's good-looking in a politician kind of way. If that's your thing.

But Raia? With her bold personality and quick mind? Her infectious laughter and locked-in determination? She's head and shoulders above the dude hiding behind her cousin.

His eyes flicker to mine and widen for a split second.

I battle my grin. Because he knows it too.

Clasping my hands together, I step toward the happy couple.

"Good to see you, Anna. Brooks." I lope my arm around Raia's waist, my hold casual.

Surprise flashes across Anna's face for a second before she steps closer. "You too, Cohen." She approaches me and gives me a kiss on the cheek before turning to her cousin. "I'm really happy you came, Rai. I hope we can…talk."

Beside me, Raia stands still. Her face is a mask, her eyes unblinking. Her cheeks are flushed and her nostrils flare. Is she going to lose it? Yell? Cry? I can't get a read on her, but I also don't want to step on her toes if she's going to make a point. Take a fucking stand against the family member and ex who did her so damn dirty.

She clears her throat lightly. Glances at me. "Lion," she mutters.

I bite the corner of my laugh to keep from grinning. My girl needs a save and I am more than happy to swoop the fuck in. "I'm sure there will be plenty of time for talking. Can you show us where we're staying first? I gotta shower and unpack after riding in that fucking clown car."

Beckett guffaws. "Dude, no fucking clue how you fit in that."

"Right?" I agree.

"Um, sure," Anna says.

"I'll show you!" Faye volunteers, grabbing Raia's arm and pulling her down the hallway.

Brooks scurries out of our way like a freaking squirrel.

"Hey, Raia," he mutters as we pass.

"Brooks," she says, her tone clipped. As she passes him, she reaches out and slaps his cheek without sparing him a second glance.

The sound of her slap reverberates in the hallway as Brooks stares after her, stunned.

Again, I fight the urge to laugh. What a fucking chump. Is he scared of her? Of me? He never deserved Raia in the first place.

"Here we are!" Faye announces brightly, pushing open the bedroom door.

We stare at the king-sized bed in the center of the bedroom. One wall is lined with windows, giving a beautiful view of the snowy mountains. There's a deck and…a small, private hot tub.

My eyes dart to Faye's and she winks. "You deserve that more than Brooks," she mutters.

I bark out a laugh and even Raia smirks.

"Take your time and settle in. We'll be in the kitchen cooking lunch when you're ready to join us," she says easily, ushering us into the bedroom and closing the door.

As her footsteps recede down the hallway, Raia's shoulders slump and she lets out a long exhale.

I see the panic cross her face right before she admits, "I'm freaking out."

"I'm proud of you for standing up for yourself." I reach for her.

Wrapping her in my arms, my chest tightens. I was hoping she'd be over Brooks and his bullshit. Is she freaking out because she misses him? If he wasn't with Anna, would she want to be with him?

The thought puts me on edge. I hate it.

"I think it's the adrenaline," she admits, sucking in a deep breath. "I've been dreading seeing them for the first time. It's...surprising even though I knew it was coming. Kind of like ripping off a Band-Aid. You know it's going to sting but you still have to pull it off."

"Oh," I say, considering her point. It makes sense even if I'd prefer for her to have zero feelings where Brooks is concerned. I kiss the top of her head. "Lion, huh?"

She laughs and nods. I hold her for another moment and then she pulls away, straightening her shoulders and heaving out an exhale. She walks deeper into the bedroom and drags her hand along the foot of the bed.

"Here's our one bed," she snorts, gesturing toward the bed frame.

I grin and wag my eyebrows. "And a private hot tub."

Raia laughs and some of the color returns to her face. "Lucky us. There's another tub on the main deck. Thanks for saving me out there, Cohen."

"Anytime, Simba."

She laughs harder. "I should've roared."

"You totally should've fucking roared. Or..." I flap my arms and make an obnoxious squawking sound.

"Oh my God!" Raia cracks up, grasping my arms. "Stop! They're going to think we're into some weird shit."

"Good." I grin. "Let them think I'm already ravaging the fuck out of you."

Raia's eyes flare as her mouth drops open. "Ravaging the fuck out of me?"

I wink. "It'll happen eventually, champ."

"Confident, are you?" She bites her bottom lip.

"Only about the things I really want. The things I'm willing to chase down."

"And you think you can catch me?" Her voice is huskier than it was a moment ago. I love that I affect her even though we both fight it. But fuck if the chemistry between us isn't blazing. Natural.

Honest.

More real than any other romantic connection I've experienced. Those were fun and fleeting, moments that never made lasting memories.

I lower my voice and drop my mouth mere millimeters from hers. "Only one way to find out."

She holds my gaze, her arms sliding from my forearms up to my shoulders. Then, she tugs me closer and presses her mouth against mine.

Our kiss is filled with the pent-up tension of the day. Her nerves and my protective edge. Her need and my fucking want.

She parts her lips and my tongue dips inside, dueling with hers. I palm her ass and grasp her upper thighs, lifting her so she can entwine her legs around my hips.

Raia moans and slants her mouth, deepening our kiss, as a knock sounds on the door.

She starts to pull away but fuck that shit. Let her friends witness how fire things are between us. I grasp the back of her head and keep her right where she is as the bedroom door swings open.

"Oh, shit," one of the guys says.

At his voice, I allow Raia to break our kiss. Glancing over her shoulder, I note Brooks's surprised expression and Beckett's shit-eating grin.

I think I'm going to like Beck too.

Raia slides down my frame and I try not to moan as she grazes over my hardening cock. I'd be mad at the interruption if I didn't get to enjoy Brooks looking embarrassed as hell.

It's almost worth having to hear him speak to Raia.

"I, uh, sorry," Brooks says, shaking his head. "I just wanted to…you know, clear the air."

"And I wanted to see if y'all were getting busy in the hot tub," Beckett admits.

Raia looks at Beckett. "It's been like five seconds."

Beckett points at me. "So? Y'all clearly move fast."

Raia rolls her eyes as I chuckle. Then, she looks at Brooks. "Yeah, Brooks, we'll clear the air. I'd like to speak with Anna too. Just, you know, maybe after lunch?"

"Sure," Brooks says quickly, his eyes darting everywhere but at Raia. And me.

My grin widens.

"Carry on," Beck says, gesturing between us.

The guys exit the room and Beck closes the door behind them.

Raia and I stare at each other for a full breath before we collapse in laughter. We hold on to each other as she hunches forward. Raia is breathless and giggling. Some of her spark is back and I revel in how beautiful she looks.

Carefree. Joyful. Perfect.

Shaking her head, she locks eyes with me, opens her mouth, and lets out the loudest raven call sound I've ever heard.

"What the fuck!" I say, repeating her words from earlier.

Then, we laugh all over again.

Raia throws her arms around me and climbs back into my hold. She kisses my cheek. "Thank you, Cohen. Thank you so much."

"I got you, champ. I promise, you and I are going to have fun this week."

"Yeah," she agrees, pulling back to grin at me. "I already am."

I smile, feeling the tightness in my chest melt at her words. My protective instincts settle and my anger over Brooks dissipates. *I'm* the guy here with Raia this weekend. *I'm* the one sharing her bed and kissing her lips. *I'm* the one earning that fucking laughter. "Me too."

FOURTEEN
RAIA

LUNCH IS MILDLY AWKWARD, with Faye and Beckett carrying the conversation. Preston occasionally chimes in, and Cohen keeps the chat on safe topics.

Anna and Brooks are silent. I'm so uncomfortable, I can barely eat. There's a phantom ache in my chest. A pull in my abdomen. A nervous energy that wraps around my fingers and pinches between my shoulder blades. It's strange to feel separate from the group I considered family for many years.

Luckily, as Cohen and Beckett clear the table, Faye gestures to the booze. "Drinks?"

"Fuck, please," Preston says, moving to grab a bottle of tequila and a bottle of gin. "Pick your poison, friends."

"Um, I don't know," Anna says nervously, glancing at me. "Maybe we should talk first?"

"Trust me, talking will be easier with some alcohol in our systems," Preston points out.

"Agreed," I add, standing and moving toward Preston. "Margaritas?"

"Done." He winks at me.

We move to the kitchen island and work in unison, squeezing limes and salting glass rims, to whip up a batch of margaritas. At the table, Faye pulls out a pack of Uno cards. I appreciate my friends trying to make this interaction normal, but the sooner I talk to Anna and Brooks, the better this trip will be.

It's going to be the toughest night, the most painful conversation. But once it's in my rearview mirror, I can enjoy the remainder of the trip with my friends and Cohen.

My eyes dart to Cohen, chatting amicably with Beck as he loads the dishwasher. God, I don't deserve him. With his backup and a strong margarita, I'm ready to take on Anna and Brooks and put the shit between us to rest.

The group assembles around the table as we play a round of Uno. Beckett wins and takes a long pull of his margarita. "We ready to hash it out?" he asks, glancing around the table.

Anna sighs and straightens in her chair. "Raia, I'm sorry."

Underneath the table, Cohen laces my hand with his. He gives a little squeeze for reassurance. I grip his fingers in return. My stomach is coiled, and I feel nauseous. A chill washes over my limbs, plunging me back to the awful moment when I learned that Brooks and Anna were dating. To seeing the picture Anna posted on social media that flipped my world upside down. To the pain of her betrayal, on top of the hurt of Brooks's rejection.

"You blindsided me," I tell Anna. My tone is clipped. My eyes dart to Brooks who is watching me curiously, his expression blank. How have I never noticed, until now, how inexpressive he is? How flat and aloof he can be? His ability to selectively engage or shut down another person is hurtful.

I used to think I was special. That I was the one person who could get through to Brooks and relate to him. That I earned his smiles and his laughter when he met everyone else with flat eyes and a simple smirk.

Now, that position is reserved for Anna.

A part of it aches but another part realizes, truly recognizes, that I'm better off. That I want to be with the guy who is affable and funny, entertaining and charismatic. I want to be with a Cohen.

Brooks clears his throat and I realize the group is waiting for me to continue. Cohen doesn't move a muscle, giving me time to gather my thoughts and bolster my confidence.

We got this. I got you.

"You both hurt me," I continue. "Well, you all did." I look around the table and note the understanding in Faye's expression as well as the surprise in Beckett's. "All I kept thinking is everyone knew, and no one told me. That Anna hid her feelings from Brooks and vice versa. Were you hooking up behind my back?"

"Never!" Anna looks truly horrified.

"Or thinking about it?" I press, glancing at Brooks. "Did you feel sorry for me? Pity me?" My gaze swings around the group.

"We would never do that, Rai." Preston's voice is low. I know he means it. Too many years being bullied as the weird outcast gave him a surprising sympathetic streak most don't realize he possesses.

I shrug. "These are the thoughts I battled this summer. You broke up with me before a huge game," I tell Brooks. "And you knew he was going to do it!" I accuse Anna.

She blushes and averts her gaze, not bothering to refute my statement. The concern she showed on the soccer field that day feels empty now. Superficial.

"I never meant to hurt you," Brooks finally says. "Not emotionally and definitely not... Raia, I was horrified when you got injured in that game."

"Yeah," I sigh, knowing he's being truthful. "So, when did it start?" I gesture between them.

"I swear, nothing happened until after you guys broke up," Anna explains. "We've been friends for so long. Brooks reached out and..." She shrugs.

"So, you rebounded with my cousin?" I narrow my eyes at Brooks.

Anna sucks in a breath, taken aback by my accusation.

Brooks looks at me, his expression carefully blank. "It's not a rebound, Rai. Anna and I have feelings for each other. Real feelings."

Cohen snorts. I lift a skeptical eyebrow. The tension hovering over the table tightens.

"We didn't know anything," Beckett promises. "I was just as surprised as you."

"I had a feeling," Faye admits. "But I didn't know anything, and I was hoping that summer would... I don't know, fix shit. I was surprised too when Brooks asked Anna out."

Cohen moves closer to me and drags our joined hands to the top of his thigh. His leg bounces restlessly.

Preston clucks his tongue and shakes his head, disappointed. "Look, this situation is messed up. What you did is pretty fucked up," he tells Brooks.

Brooks shifts uncomfortably.

"And y'all are fucking family," he says to Anna, giving another voice to my points. God, I love Pres. "But," he continues, "we've been friends for a long time."

"Family," Beckett corrects.

"Family," Preston agrees. "We gotta find a way to move through this. Even if it's awkward."

"Oh, it's awkward," Faye agrees, and we laugh lightly. A nervous, uncomfortable tittering among friends who used to share their deepest secrets.

The nausea in my stomach rolls.

"I wish you would have told me the truth," I say to Anna. "I would have preferred to hear about your dating Brooks from *you*, not your social media. The fact that you couldn't be bothered with having the conversation hurt."

"I was planning on telling you!" Anna swears. "I just, I

didn't know how. I was scared of the fallout between us and our families. About our team. I waited too long and… I'm so sorry I hurt you, Raia. You're like a sister to me and I hate that I caused this." She gestures around the table and the tension hovering overhead like a raincloud. Tears coat her eyes, and she blinks rapidly to keep them from falling.

"You should've reached out before you posted a picture on your socials," Preston scoffs.

I give him a grateful look, but his gaze is trained on Anna.

"You're right," she sniffs. "I should have."

"I'm sorry too, Rai," Brooks says, staring right at me. "My timing was shitty, and I should have handled the situation better. But I want to ask you something. I want you to be honest."

Cohen shifts again, leaning forward slightly.

Brooks shakes his head. "I'm asking this in front of our friends, in front of Anna, because I want you to tell me the truth. Don't spare my feelings."

"Don't worry about that," I mutter.

One side of Brooks's mouth pulls up. "Were you happy with me? Truly happy? Or did you just feel comfortable? Was our relationship easy and on paper, it made sense?"

Shit. I lean back in my chair and stare at the table. A few months ago, I would have sworn that I was happy and in love with Brooks.

But things are different now. I'm sitting here, with Cohen at my side. Through him and my experience with him, I learned that what Brooks and I shared doesn't measure up. My fake boyfriend outshines the man I spent a decade dating.

"It was easy, and I was comfortable," I admit.

Cohen lets out a shaky exhale and his body relaxes. Was he worried? Does he think I'm hung up on Brooks? I'm not.

I squeeze Cohen's hand in reassurance. In solidarity.

The realization that I truly am over my ex-boyfriend

makes me chuckle. "But I didn't want to admit it," I continue, "because I still feel betrayed by both of you."

"You should," Brooks agrees. "We handled it wrong because we didn't want to hurt you, Rai."

"I miss you," Anna says, one tear rolling down her cheek. She swipes it away and sniffles. "I miss you so much. Part of me hates myself for what I put you through and the other part is so happy because Brooks makes me happy, and I don't know how to reconcile that." She winces. "Shit, I'm sorry. That was an insensitive and fucked-up thing to say."

"Ya think?" Preston snorts.

"No, it's fine. At least it's honest. We should aim for more honesty in our group." I look at my cousin. Really look at her and see the girl who's been my ride or die my entire life. "I miss you, too," I say truthfully. "But it's going to take time to…trust this again." I gesture between us.

She nods. "I understand."

Beckett leans forward, resting his elbows on the table. "You guys, this is so healthy. When the fuck did we grow up and become adults who can talk through shit?"

"Uh, thirteen minutes ago," Faye replies, glancing at her watch.

The table laughs as the tension diffuses. The energy in the room shifts as relief courses through our group.

"Consider the air cleared," I tell Anna and Brooks.

Preston gives me a surprised look.

I squeeze Cohen's hand again. "Honestly, if I wasn't with Cohen, if we weren't so happy, I probably wouldn't be this forgiving." As I say the words, I know they're true. I moved on from Brooks partly because Cohen showed me something better. "And I don't want this trip to be awkward. We hardly get to spend time together as a group and I want to enjoy this."

Anna nods as Brooks tips his chin at me.

"Okay, Rai, slow your roll. You can be an adult, but you don't have to be so goddamn mature about it," Beckett jokes.

I chuckle and pick up my margarita. "To the tribe."

"To our family," Preston says, following my lead.

"And welcome to Cohen," Beckett tacks on.

We lift our glasses, clink them together, and down them.

"That was intense," Cohen whispers as Preston makes another round of margaritas.

"Yeah," I agree, scrunching my nose. "But annoyingly healthy."

"I thought you were going to do that, you know, just you and Anna. Not the whole group…"

I shrug. "We're all ride or die. We've been up in each other's business and on our own, without our parents to police things, for too long."

Cohen nods. "Makes sense. You have a really special friendship."

"Yeah," I agree, glancing at Anna and Brooks who are huddled together on the sofa.

"I'm proud of you, champ. That wasn't easy and you handled that shit with a lot more grace than I'd be capable of." Cohen squeezes my thigh.

I glance at him and grin. "It was easier with you here."

He smiles back. "Always got your back, Rai."

"I know," I reply. And I trust that.

Deep down, I know everyone at this table has my back. Even when it hurts.

FIFTEEN
COHEN

"YOU'RE GOOD FOR HER," Beckett tells me as we split logs for the fireplace.

"You think?" I cock my head, curious for his take on the situation.

"Yeah." He brings down the axe, expertly splitting the wood.

Shit. Is this something they learned at boarding school? I have no clue how to do any of this outdoorsy, lumberjack stuff. Does Brooks?

I shake the thought away. Raia's over him; she said it a few hours ago. While she was holding my hand.

Beck gathers the wood and looks at me. "This situation has been tough to navigate. Brooks and Raia have been together for years. They were kind of a permanent fixture. The last few months, with her being MIA, man, I was fucking worried about her. Raia's got a big personality. She loves hard and when she hurts, it's deep. But seeing her with you, man, she's happy. She's got this spark I haven't realized she lost until I saw it again. That's all you, dude." He points at me. "Now don't fuck it up because I like you."

I laugh, caught off guard by his honesty more than his warning. "It's all her, man. She's...she's a champion," I admit, realizing the nickname I've used for years is true. Raia always rises above and comes out victorious. She puts in the work and is so unflinchingly honest in her approach. "She impresses the hell out of me."

"Bet," Beckett agrees. "We've all been friends a long time and if you asked me a year ago, I would have said she and Brooks were perfect together. But now"—he shakes his head—"you're the type of guy she should be with. Brooks stopped challenging her a long time ago and Anna..." He sighs. "Well, Anna is tired of being challenged so Brooks is a good fit for her. I'm just glad the group is intact. I can't lose those fuckers."

I snort. "Yeah, I sense that. I've never seen friends as close as you guys. Avery is my best friend, and we have a long history, but when he and Mila broke up, it ruined our friend group."

"Raia and Anna have the most stable families of our crew. The rest of us, we need the foundation of our friendships to anchor us. Without this"—he gestures toward the house and the people playing charades through the living room window—"I'd be lost at sea, praying to drown." He gives me a sad smile but doesn't elaborate and I don't push.

If anything, I appreciate how upfront he's been.

"Raia has you. She's got Avery. Hell, even her parents could help her navigate. As worried as I was about her, I knew I didn't have to rush to Knoxville. If it had been Faye..." He shrugs. "Different story, you know?"

"Yeah," I say even though I don't know. My parents and Cooper would do anything for me and vice versa. Not to mention Avery, Mila, and Maisy Stratford. I guess I have a solid crew too. I just never recognized—or appreciated—it as much as Raia's friends do.

I follow Beckett back to the house and we kick off our boots and shrug out of our winter coats. Then, Brooks builds a fire, Preston whips up more cocktails, and we hang out, playing charades that gradually turn into drinking games until midnight.

Faye's the first to yawn. "We should crash if we're going to hit the slopes early tomorrow," she says, dragging a hand across her eyes.

"Yeah," Preston agrees, standing from the couch. He stumbles slightly and Faye snorts.

"Easy there, mate," Brooks advises.

Anna giggles and Brooks helps her up. They wander down a hallway to their bedroom. "Good night, everyone." Anna waves before slipping inside her room.

Faye rolls her eyes. Beckett tosses her over his shoulder.

"Beck! Stop it!" She laughs, pounding on his back.

"You took two shots too many," he reminds her, carrying her to bed.

"You guys good?" Preston asks.

"Yeah. We're great," Raia confirms.

"'Kay. Good night," Preston says.

"Night, man," I reply, pulling myself up. As soon as I stand, the room tilts. Shit, I didn't think the alcohol would hit me this hard.

I'm not drunk but definitely tipsy. I glance at Raia.

She giggles and waves. She's drunk.

"Want me to carry you to bed?" I offer, lifting an eyebrow.

"I want you to do a lot more than that," she admits, rolling her lips together.

I laugh and bend to scoop her up. I carry her fireman style over the threshold of our bedroom, kick the door shut, and lay her in the center of the bed.

"Are you having fun?" I ask as my eyes adjust to the darkness.

She bites her bottom lip and nods slowly. "More than I thought. I really did miss my friends."

"I know." I brush my thumb across her cheek. "They missed you too."

"Thanks for coming with me, Cohen. For doing this." She waves an arm around the room.

"This got a lot more complicated than it was supposed to," I mutter, spilling a truth.

"Yeah," she replies, her eyes darkening. "But I'm not sorry."

"Neither am I."

Raia widens her legs on the bed and reaches for me. I dip forward, my fists landing on the soft mattress. Raia's palm slides behind my neck as she guides my mouth to hers and I fall into her kiss.

She tastes like tequila and lime. She smells like winter. And she feels like a fucking wonderland. She leans back until she's lying on her back, her arms around my neck, her breasts pressing into my chest.

I kiss her deep and slow, wanting to savor this night with her.

Tonight, I learned more about Raia Callaway. Her loyalty and grace. Her sweetness and ferocity. And fuck if spending time away from Knoxville with her isn't messing with my head.

Things are more than complicated.

They're intoxicating. She's intoxicating.

Her knees fall to the sides as I settle firmly between them. My hand slides up Raia's abdomen and I drag her shirt over her head, discarding it on the floor.

"You're beautiful, champ," I murmur. Her bra is a deep blue and the prettiest pink nipples flash through the delicate lace cup. Dipping my head, I flick my tongue over her nipple before pulling the tip of her breast into my mouth. My tongue moves lazily over the lace as I trace her areola.

Raia moans, her hand clutching the back of my head.

Slowly, I drag my mouth to her other peak and give it the same attention. Then, I kiss a path down the center of her chest, over her abdomen, until my chin rests at the top of her leggings.

I look at her, loving her hooded eyes and flushed cheeks.

"Take this off," she commands, reaching for my shirt.

I pull it off in one tug.

"Lift," I demand, tapping her hip. She acquiesces.

I roll her leggings down and drop them next to her shirt. Then I fucking groan because her thong is the same delicate blue lace as her bra and she looks delectable in it.

"You were wearing this all day," I state the obvious.

"Mm-hmm," she sighs. "I was hoping we'd end up here."

I grin at her wickedly. Trace a finger lightly over her core. She bucks at my touch and her arousal dampens my fingertip.

"Thinking about this all day?" I wonder, repeating my movement.

"Since I woke up this morning," she admits, her voice breathy.

"You're wet for me, Rai," I tell her, nibbling on her inner thigh.

Her hand finds my hair again. "How do you know?"

"Can feel it," I say, stroking the pad of my thumb over the strip of lace in a slow rhythm.

"Wanna taste it?" she taunts.

A growl sounds in back of my throat. Of course, I want to fucking taste her. I've been dying to since the first time she kissed me. But we haven't done that yet. We haven't crossed that line.

I look up at her. Love the fucking challenge that sparks in her eyes.

"More than I wanna breathe."

She giggles but it's husky. Needy.

"Baby, this changes things," I warn. If I thought shit was complicated, this is going to cause tangles and double knots.

"Good." Her voice is firm.

I scrape my teeth lightly over her inner thigh again, hook my finger around her thong, and tug it to the side. Fuck, her pussy looks so damn delicious. "You sure?"

"Yes."

"Look at me," I demand.

She gives me her beautiful gray eyes. I keep my gaze on her as I drag my tongue up her center.

Raia's body shudders and she lets out the sexiest moan I've ever heard. She's up on her elbows but her head is dropped back and the moonlight ripples over her frame, making the visual just as sexy as the act.

"So fucking sweet," I mutter, snapping her thong at her hip and discarding the lace. Then, I wrap my arms underneath her legs, splay my palms on her lower abdomen, and lick her pussy the way I've been denying myself.

Desperately. Completely.

Her back arches off the bed, but I hold her steady as I lick her core, suck on her clit, and nibble on her sensitive flesh. I keep my strokes long and deep, followed by short and shallow, working my girl up.

"Cohen," she gasps, both her hands tugging my hair. Driving me wild. Her breathing intensifies. "Cohen, don't stop."

"Never," I promise.

I pull one hand back so I can slip two fingers into her channel.

She swears, the sound half strangled. I fucking grin.

Then, I pump into her, setting a steady pace, as I devour her clit.

Her inner thighs shake and her breathing grows frantic.

"So good, baby," I murmur against her pussy. "Taste so

fucking good." I blow on her lightly and she cries out. Then, I drag my tongue up her core again and Raia shatters.

Her orgasm rocks her tight body, and she moans my name in the sexiest tone I've ever heard. I continue to kiss her hips and stomach, her pert breasts, and the side of her neck as she comes down from her high. Then, I turn her face toward mine and kiss her lips, sliding my tongue inside so she can taste how fucking sweet she is.

The action turns me on more and my length, hard as a steel pipe, brushes against her hip and sends a shudder through my body.

"Ooh," Raia murmurs, reaching for me. She kisses me recklessly as her hand fists my cock and begins to pump.

"Fuck, Rai," I swear. "You don't have to—"

"I want to," she cuts me off.

"Raia, I—"

"I got you, Cohen." Her tone is decisive, her eyes clear. She nudges me onto my back, and I roll over. Staring up at her, I reach for her face. She leans into my palm before pressing a kiss to the center of it.

Then, she works her way down my frame. Her hair tickles my chest and I gather it in my hand, holding it away from her face as she takes my cock in between her plush lips.

"Oh, fuck," I swear, dragging out the word as Raia begins to bob her head.

Fuck doesn't cover it. The visual of Raia taking me in and out is enough to cause my body to tighten.

What the hell is happening?

It's never been like this before. This fast, this needy, this fucking explosive.

"Slow down, Rai," I mutter, scared I'll blow my load too soon. But she's performing straight up voodoo on my dick, and I can't control how my body splinters at the seams.

Raia gets her hand into the mix, fisting my base as she

sucks the tip. She licks at me like a goddamn lollipop, and I dig my free hand into the duvet. "Raia, fuck, baby, fuck."

"You like that?" she taunts.

"A lot," I groan.

"Me too," she murmurs, holding my eyes as she licks up my shaft and pulls my tip into her mouth. She places a light kiss on the head and my eyes roll back in my head.

Raia laughs and sets a steady pace. In mere minutes, my balls tighten, the base of my spine tingles, and I know it's no use. "Baby, I'm gonna come."

She doesn't stop sucking.

"Raia," I warn her again. "I'm gonna—fuck." Ribbons of my desire, hot and thick, coat her tongue and she doesn't fucking stop. "Oh, fuck," I swear again, unable to say any other word.

Raia sucks me clean, swallowing my want, and licking her lips when she's done. She grins at me, straddling my legs and giving me another glimpse of her pretty, swollen pussy. "You taste good too, Cohen."

"Fuck me," I reply, staring at the ceiling.

Raia giggles and drops next to me. I pull her into my side, and she rests her head on my shoulder.

"Raia, that was... There are no words."

"Except *fuck*," she supplies.

I snort in agreement. She snuggles deeper and presses a kiss to my cheek.

"That was fun, Cohen," she murmurs.

"We're not done yet."

"We're not?"

I shake my head, trying to muster some strength. Then, I stand, pick Raia up, and carry her into the bathroom. I flip on the shower, wait for the water to heat, and pull Raia into the shower with me.

I wash her body, dragging my palms along every curve. I scrub her hair, loving her laughter as I rinse the conditioner from her chocolate strands. I wash quickly so I can wrap her in a big, fluffy towel, and carry her back to bed.

"I don't deserve you," she teases.

I shake my head, staring at her. "You deserve all good things, champ."

Her expression softens and she opens her arms. I go willingly. Wrapped in her embrace, I drift off to sleep. Naked but warm. Sated but wanting.

And happier than I've been in a long fucking time.

THE COLD WIND whips past as I ski down the hill. White powder, blue skies, and the laughter of my friends echoing in my eardrums. My body feels strong, that insatiable itch for movement momentarily silenced by the stunning views and adrenaline pumping through my veins.

It feels incredible to push my body again.

It feels unbelievable to start my morning with Cohen's kiss lingering on my lips.

The hours melt into each other as I find my groove on the slopes.

"You're happy," Faye says as we pull down the bar of the chairlift.

I smirk at her. "It's new."

"Yes and no," she replies. "There's history there."

I shrug. "He used to see me as his kid sister."

"Ages ago. Rai, you've always had a thing for Cohen."

I widen my eyes at her, recalling the secret I confessed to Anna a million years ago. It was our first year at boarding school, before I was dating Brooks. I was homesick, and Cohen sent me a box of brownies during mid-term exams. "I only told Anna that."

Faye giggles gleefully, pumping a fist in the air. "So, I'm right?!"

My mouth drops open. "You were bluffing?"

"It was an educated guess…based on the evidence before me." She points at me. "So, there's history."

"Yes," I agree, rolling my lips together. "There's history."

"And you're happy?" This time, it's asked as a question instead of said as a statement. Good ol' Faye, always looking out.

"Yes, Faye. I'm happy."

My friend squeals again, bumping her shoulder against mine. "I'm thrilled for you, Rai. He's a good guy. And the fact that Avery isn't flipping you shit? It means your family adores him, too."

Avery. The mention of my brother causes guilt to coat my stomach. "Yep," I reply, trying to cross my fingers inside my gloves as I lie to my friend. Still, I sidestep the biggest elephant at the ski resort.

Cohen and I are frauds.

Our relationship is fake.

Except…it isn't.

"Let's do this!" Faye cheers as our lift reaches the top of the next hill.

I follow her down the mountain, trying to lose myself in the run. In the moment.

But my thoughts keep turning back to Cohen.

Are we making a mistake?

Is this going to blow up in our faces?

Am I willing to shut it down now to avoid a future disaster?

No! The word rings in my head.

I feel heartsick at the idea, which means, I'm in too deep.

I should end things in order to protect myself. Not to mention Avery's friendship with his best friend. Besides, I'm moving to Spain and all athletes know long-distance relationships rarely last.

I shouldn't think of myself as the exception when the rule is clear.

Put the sport first. Everything else is secondary.

Gah! I sigh as I finish the run, annoyed with myself for being too distracted to appreciate it. For torturing myself with thoughts of Cohen and our confusing attachment.

Knowing I'll spend the remainder of the morning lost in my thoughts, I lift a hand to Faye and head back to the ski chalet.

Since Cohen can't risk his contract, he stayed behind. Right now, I want to see him. Speak with him.

Kiss him.

And that's a problem.

Surprise crosses Cohen's face when I enter the kitchen. "You're back early."

I don't respond. Can't form words. My throat is parched, my eyes dry from a sudden inability to blink.

Because Cohen Campbell is standing in the kitchen, bare-foot and bare chested, with only a pair of cream joggers draping oh-so-low on his hips. There's a V. He has the goddamn V.

And he's cooking.

Are you fucking kidding me?

"Where's your shirt?" I rasp.

He chuckles and turns toward me fully, dropping a spatula on the countertop. "Just finished working out."

"Shirtless?" I gawk.

His abdomen is ridge after ridge. Like mountains.

His shoulders are broad and strong. Like bridges.

And don't get me started on that V…

"Shirtless," he confirms, tilting his head. "Like what you see?"

"Hmm," I neither confirm nor deny.

Cohen's smile widens. He's amused and playful and so sexy, especially because the next words out of his mouth are, "You hungry?"

For what? my mind wonders.

"Uh-huh," my mouth sputters.

"I made pancakes," he clarifies.

Of course, he did.

"Blueberry and chocolate chip," he continues, drizzling maple syrup on a short stack.

Then, he gestures toward the table. "Why don't you get comfortable, and we'll eat together."

"'Kay," I wheeze. Wheeze!

I hustle to our bedroom with Cohen's chuckle following me. I don't care how embarrassed I *should* be. Because I'm not embarrassed at all.

Instead, I change into a little green bikini, ahem, it's mostly strings, and toss a charcoal-colored sweater on top.

I push the warnings from the slopes out of my mind.

Instead, I focus on Cohen, pancakes, and the big hot tub that beckons from the deck outside the large, sliding doors.

There are too many views to ogle.

Cohen's seated at the table. Two plated stacks of pancakes, decorated with fruit, and drizzled with maple syrup, as well as mugs of coffee await.

I blush, touched by his thoughtfulness. "Thanks for making me pancakes."

"I'm glad you're here to share them with," he quips.

I sit across from him and dip my head as we cut into our pancakes.

"How was skiing?"

"Wonderful," I admit, gushing as I tell him about the sweeping views.

He frowns slightly, his eyebrows bending and the subtlest

crease dipping in between his magnetic eyes. "You didn't have to come back on my account."

"I didn't," I sigh.

He lifts a questioning brow.

"Well, not entirely," I amend.

Cohen's frown deepens and I squirm in my chair, pressing my thighs together. My gaze flickers to the hot tub.

"You don't have to worry about—"

"I missed you," I cut him off.

He pauses, his eyes regarding me curiously.

Shit.

"And I wanted to…" Again, I look out at the deck.

Cohen follows my gaze. His eyes snap back to mine. Disbelief washes over his expression and his grip on the fork tightens.

Shit. Shit. Shit.

"We don't have to—"

"How hungry are you?" he cuts me off.

I smile slowly and slip my sweater off my shoulder to show him the strap of my bathing suit. "I'm already wearing a bikini."

Cohen nods once and then, he's clamoring from his seat and rushing to our bedroom.

"Wait! Your pancakes are gonna get cold!" I call after him.

"Who gives a fuck?" is his muffled reply.

I laugh and eat a few bites.

I close my eyes and savor the taste. They're good. Just like the man who made them.

When I open my eyes, Cohen's standing before me in bright orange swim trunks decorated with bananas.

I snort, my hand clapping over my mouth.

He grins. "Knew you'd get a kick out of these."

"Did you buy them?"

"What do you think?" he tosses back.

"Who'd you lose a bet to?" I giggle.

"Gage," we say in unison, both releasing our nervous tension with laughter.

I point at his plate. "You sure you don't want to eat?"

He shakes his head, his eyes never leaving mine. "Not when something sweeter is on the menu."

I groan at his lame joke.

His grin widens. "You love my humor."

I stand from my chair and walk around the table, taking his outstretched hand. "Whatever you tell yourself, Cohen."

"I tell myself a lot, champ."

Before I can decipher the meaning behind his words, he's pulling me toward the deck.

"Wait here," he says as he rushes out into the freezing temperature to remove the cover, check the water, and start the jets. Then, he beckons for me to join him.

"Oh, God!" I exclaim, shivering in my string bikini. "It's freezing!"

Cohen doesn't reply and when I look up, I realize why.

"You check me out that hard, your eyes are gonna get stuck," I joke.

"You're cold," he replies, his eyes on my chest. I snort. "Don't worry," he rumbles in my ear, lifting me up and carrying me—like a freaking feather—into the tub. "I'll warm you up."

It's a lame joke but I don't laugh because his hot mouth is trailing down my neck, peppering my skin with open-mouthed kisses, and I sigh in contentment.

As I drop my head back, my arms tighten around his neck. Cohen holds me closer, the foam from the bubbles enveloping us. My legs twist around him and as he moves, pressing me into the corner of the hot tub, his hardness brushes against my core.

"Already?" I whisper.

"Been ready, babe," he replies, pulling back to look at me. "Been waiting."

Then, his mouth is on mine.

There is no joking. No playful laughter. No banter.

There's only this.

Me and Cohen and an endless winter wonderland.

There's only us.

SEVENTEEN
COHEN

"IT'S GETTING PRETTY steamy in there," a male voice calls out.

And motherfucking hell, I stop.

I stop grinding my erection against Raia's perfect pussy. I refrain from dragging my mouth along the column of her neck. I release the strands of her hair fisted in my hands.

"You've gotta be kidding me," she pants, her breath warm against my cheek.

I groan, falling forward into her arms and pressing my forehead against her shoulder.

A slow clap fills the air and I know it's Preston. Beckett would've cheered me on. He would've eagerly upheld bro code.

Raia's shoulders tremble and I know she's holding back laughter. I sputter, shaking my head in disbelief.

I pull away from Raia, and glare at the punk behind me.

He fucking grins.

Beside him, Faye is laughing uncontrollably. Her shoulders shake, tears pooling at the corners of her eyes, but no sounds erupt.

"You okay?" I ask her.

"Are you?" she volleys, her laughter breaking the air.

I snort and shake my head. Glancing down, I admit, "Not really."

We all crack up, realizing that Raia and I have been completely interrupted and I've gotta get my shit under control since I'm not going to get lucky in the hot tub. At least, not right this moment.

"We'll give y'all a minute," Faye says, grasping Preston's elbow and leading him into the chalet.

"Real generous of you," I call after her.

She chuckles again.

Shaking my head, I glance at Raia.

She presses her lips together, her expression sympathetic. Gliding over to me, she palms my erection and I jerk away.

"You're not helping," I rasp out.

She bites her bottom lip and I groan. Why is she doing this to me?

"This is torture," I tack on.

"Maybe I could help?" she offers, her voice seductive.

"Not now," I declare, my gaze darting back to the kitchen and the large sliding glass doors, and her friends' watchful eyes.

Raia shrugs. "I guess it'd be messed up if we took things too far in this hot tub, huh? I mean, it is for everyone, and we have our own."

"Right now, I don't give a fuck about anyone but you," I admit, not caring how selfish that is. Up until a few minutes ago, I couldn't think about anything but getting Raia Callaway naked.

And now, the scent of her hair is tickling my nostrils. The curves of her hips are imprinted on my palms. The need I have for her is rushing through my veins, pumping in my bloodstream.

I have to shut this down.

"I need to take a cold shower," I decide.

She tilts her head. "You could jump in the snow."

"For fuck's sake." That's the last thing I feel like doing.

She reaches out a hand. "I'll go with you."

"What?" I gape at her. "You want to jump in the snow?"

"Come on, Cohen! It'll be fun. Hilarious. A story." Her tone is teasing, but I know she's serious.

"This isn't like a Swedish spa with the hot baths and cold plunges," I remind her, giving her an out.

"I know. This is an adventure. Me and you."

God, who is this woman? "Me and you," I repeat. Taking her hand, I lace our fingers together and pull her to the edge of the hot tub. Then, I drop her hand and palm her ass. Cop one last feel before I mentally commit to throwing myself into a goddamn snowbank.

"Let me help you out," I command, swinging my leg over the ledge of the hot tub.

Raia's breath catches, and her eyes widen. She's checking out my junk since I'm pitching a tent. But there's no time for me to be embarrassed. Not when it's freezing cold and her friends are on the floor, laughing at us. I scoop my girl out of the tub.

Raia's arms intertwine around my neck. She presses her pretty titties against my chest, and I pray that small scrap of a triangle moves a few inches to the right.

"Cohen!" Raia yells.

I run across the deck, calling out a war cry and spin at the last second, to ensure I drop into a mound of snow but keep Raia as untouched by the powder as possible.

"Fuck!" I wheeze. Icy jolts shock my system, cooling off the passion that burned bright seconds earlier. Small miracles.

Above me, Raia beams. Dancing gray eyes and a wide smile, she tosses her head back and laughs. It's so pure and carefree that I pause, drinking her in.

My heart skips a beat and my admiration for this woman

multiplies. How did I get so lucky to have this moment with her?

"Come on! You're going to get hypothermia!" Faye hollers from the sliding doors.

Raia nods, yanking on my arm. I stand and shake off the snow.

"You're like a lion," Raia jokes.

"Yeah. I'll be your lion," I shoot back.

She groans. "We need to work on your game, babe."

"Why? It got me you."

Her eyes shimmer.

"No comeback?" I taunt.

She shakes her head and bites that sexy bottom lip.

I smirk and tap her ass. "Let's go. I'll race you back!" I take off at a jog but, of course, Raia rises to the challenge and sprints ahead.

I let her win just so she can rub it in my face.

I've never craved a woman's bullshit as much as I love Raia's.

I've never desired a woman the way I want her.

Even more than football.

That night, over dinner, my eyes keep straying to Raia. I notice things I've never cared to spot before. The roses that bloom in her cheeks when she sips her wine. The tilt of her head when she considers one of her friend's thoughts on a subject. How she claps her hands together when something is truly funny.

Nuances. Slivers of her personality. Tiny things that, when combined, comprise the woman she is. A woman I have true, deep feelings for.

A woman who I once treated like a little sister.

A woman who is leaving Tennessee.

My chest aches at the reminder, a longing echo already filling the space even though she's here, sitting across the table with moonbeams in her eyes.

"You guys are gross," Beckett accuses us good-naturedly.

Anna smiles softly. She's been hesitant around her cousin, treading lightly while trying to make inroads. "I like it. You look happy, Rai."

Raia gives her a nod and bites that bottom lip.

Brooks sighs heavily. "Well, I hate to be the bearer of bad news."

"Bullshit," Beckett scoffs. "That's your forte."

Faye snorts.

Brooks rolls his eyes. "There's a storm coming in."

Preston stills. "How bad?"

Anna winces, her eyes darting to Brooks before turning to her friends. "We need to cut our trip short." She wrinkles her nose, apologetic.

Brooks reaches for her hand, and Raia zeroes in on the gesture. But she doesn't react. That's progress.

My shoulders relax and I lean back in my chair.

"Shit," Beckett whistles, staring at his phone screen. "This snowstorm is no joke. Flights are gonna be grounded for sure."

"Damn," Preston mutters. "I may need to leave early, too."

"Why?" Faye arches an eyebrow.

Preston blushes slightly and the entire table hunches closer, as if to extract this information from him. He shifts uncomfortably. "I have an interview."

"An interview?" Faye asks.

"With whom?" Brooks demands.

Preston shakes his head. "Can't say."

"Ooh, some international spy organization," Anna surmises.

Raia claps her hands together. "The US Government. It's the government, isn't it?"

Preston chuckles and shrugs, not giving a straight answer.

"Well, I'm doing whatever you're doing," Faye says. "I need to crash at yours for a few days."

"Still avoiding your family?" Anna asks.

"Is it called avoiding when they don't realize you're not there?" Faye's tone is sarcastic, and I catch the undercurrent of hurt.

Damn, Raia wasn't kidding about how tight her crew rolls.

"This sucks," Beckett laments.

"Let's see what the morning brings. If we need to make changes, we will," Faye advises.

"What about you two?" Anna asks Raia and me.

Raia shrugs, her eyes latching onto mine. I see the excitement in her irises.

We could have this whole place to ourselves, they announce.

I know, mine smile back.

Beckett groans again.

"Y'all should be fine," Faye shares, showing us her screen. "You're flying south so your flight shouldn't be affected."

I shrug, feigning nonchalance. "We'll see how tomorrow looks."

Anna and Raia share a secret smile and my heart warms that they're falling back into their old groove. As much as Raia was gutted over Brooks, losing Anna cut deeper.

"If this is our last night..." Preston relocates to the booze.

"Bring it on, Pres!" Faye agrees.

Raia laughs, leaning back in her chair and polishing off her wine glass.

She looks so relaxed and comfortable in this moment. Confident in who she is and happy about where she's at. In her presence, I can envision my whole damn future.

Me and her. A family. A home.

And it scares the fucking hell out of me, which only makes me want it more.

I shake my head as Beckett grabs Twister.

"No way," Faye agrees.

"Let's play a drinking game," Preston suggests.

"What is it with you and the booze on this trip?" Anna asks.

Preston shrugs, averting his gaze.

A flicker of unease crosses Raia's face and I reach for her, pulling her into my side. I kiss her temple, reveling in the feel of her petite frame under my arm.

I love how much she cares about her friends. I love how giving and generous she is with her attention and affection.

She puts up a fiery exterior, but on the inside, my girl is all honey. Sweet, soothing, and golden.

I fight the urge to kiss her again. I'm laying it on thick but it's no longer for her friends' sakes or to help her save face. It's because I can't keep my hands to myself.

I'm desperate to finish what we started in the hot tub earlier today. Especially now that our trip may end early. I want as many seconds with Raia as I can steal. And I certainly don't want to spend them playing fucking Twister.

Raia rolls her lips together and glances at me. Her gray eyes are charcoal, laced with heat.

"What are you thinking?" I murmur.

"Exactly what you're thinking."

I smirk. "What do you want to do about it?"

"Take care of it," she replies, standing up and tugging me with her.

"Where are you—" Preston starts but then he shakes his head. "Nope, not going there."

"Yeahhhhh, Rai! Get it, girl!" Beckett hollers, doing a ridiculous dance.

"Don't ever do that in public again," Faye tells him.

I give her a high five and Raia laughs.

"Good night, guys. We're turning in," Raia announces.

"You know, in case we have to travel early because of the

storm," I attempt to find an explanation that isn't centered on how badly I want to get Raia in between the sheets.

Her friends erupt in laughter.

"Don't try to lie," Faye warns me. "You're not good at it."

I snort in agreement and let Raia drag me to the bedroom.

Once the door clicks behind us, her joking morphs into a seriousness, a sensuality, that pulls me up short.

This is happening; this is for real.

Raia drops my hand and spins to stare at me. Outside our window, moonlight reflects off the snow, bathing her in a soft glow.

She slips off her sweatpants and loses her hoodie. Standing before me in a charcoal bra and thong, she smiles. "You have me, Cohen. Now, what're you going to do with me?"

I drink her in, my eyes savoring every inch of her skin. "Worship the hell out of this hot body," I admit, skimming my palm down her arm. My other hand hooks around her waist and pulls her closer. "And love on you so damn good, Rai."

EIGHTEEN
RAIA

COHEN'S WORDS cause a thrill to skate over my skin. His eyes darken, hunger and want shadowing his irises. The stubble on his jaw is sexy and when he rubs his palm over his chin, the sound erupts in the air like tiny fireworks.

Every part of my body is on high alert. I ache for the drag of his tongue down the column of my neck, for the nip of his teeth on my hips, and to feel arousal pulse and pool between my thighs.

How can he unravel me with one look? With simple words? He's barely touched me and I'm nearly ready to detonate. Or melt. I don't care which as long as it's with him.

"Show me," I murmur, my voice throaty.

Cohen's hand fists the ends of my hair, and he tugs lightly so my face lifts. "Look at me," he commands.

I do.

"This means something, champ. This means something big." His eyes search mine, confirming that I want to take this leap. Trust in him and the future.

"Show me," I repeat.

Relief and regret both flicker his expression. Before I can read into either, his mouth descends on mine. His mouth is soft, his want hard. His lips pry mine open and his tongue dips inside to dance with mine.

I hook my hands on his shoulders to pull myself closer and when his erection grinds into my stomach, he sucks on my tongue and I groan.

Cohen cups my cheeks, angles my head, and kisses me deeper. His kisses ride an emotional wave of desire, need, and want with an undercurrent of affection and respect. It's heady and intoxicating as much as reassuring and caressing.

He makes my head spin and my heart gallop.

I grasp his wrists and feel his mouth curve into a smile against the corner of mine. "I got you, love."

Love. I sigh.

He savors.

Cohen continues to kiss and touch, his thumbs brushing arcs over my cheekbones, his palms skimming my cheeks, as he relocates us to the bed. He lays me down, drinks me in, and lets loose with a litany of swears that sound like a prayer.

I blush at his dirty words, and he shakes his head. Then, he grips his shirt behind his neck and rips it off in one sharp tug.

My tongue hits the center of my bottom lip as I take in the glory of his body. Hard ridges, abs for days, muscles that coil and roll in his shoulders.

My hands lift and I dust my palms over his smooth pecs. He dips over me and catches my palm, anchoring it to his chest. His heart beats steady and soothing against my hand.

"This is different," he states, his eyes boring into mine. "You're different, Rai."

"So are you."

"I've never... I've never done this before and felt this much."

I shiver. His words slay me. How can he be so honest? Vulnerable?

How can he want me?

"Cohen," I murmur.

He shakes his head, my arm folding between us as he practically lowers himself into a pushup, hovering inches over my frame. "Don't say anything, Rai. I just want you to know: being with you, it's everything."

He kisses me again and I open for him. My lips part and my knees fall to the sides. I accommodate his body between my legs, and he wastes no time dragging his mouth down to my chest.

His touch is sure but his pace is exploratory. It's like he wants to kiss and touch and memorize every inch of my body. It's like he's scared he won't get to do it again tomorrow.

But he will. I'll let him do this every damn day.

I arch up as he tugs the cup of my bra down, trussing up my breast. The cold air causes my nipple to pebble, and he flicks his tongue over the point. The heat from his mouth chases the goose bumps on my skin and I groan again, fisting his hair.

He sucks my breast into his mouth and lavishes it with his attention. My legs open wider, and he grinds even closer. The space between us becomes nonexistent as we melt together in a dance, a rhythm, that's more natural than breathing.

With Cohen, I'm not self-conscious or anticipating what comes next. No, I'm wholly in the moment, letting his touch consume me.

His mouth travels to my other breast before his hands squeeze my waist and he moves lower. The scrape of his teeth along my ribs, the lightning-fast flick of his tongue over my belly button, the heat of his mouth against my core.

"Cohen," I warble as he hooks my legs over his shoulders.

He grins at me, a playful expression with bedroom eyes, as his knees hit the floor and he drags me to the edge of the bed.

"Let me eat, Rai."

I shiver.

"Gonna devour this sweet pussy," he continues, dragging two fingers over my slit.

His touch is painstakingly slow, and I buck against it.

Cohen grabs my thighs and holds them open. He runs his tongue over the seam of my thong, pressing the rough lace over my sensitive folds.

"Oh, God," I mutter.

He does it again. And again.

On the fourth pass, he snaps my thong at the hip and lets it fall away.

"Uh," I stutter, sitting up on my elbows. "Again?"

"I'll buy you more," he promises.

Before I can make a fuss, his mouth is on my clit. His tongue is in me. The sound of him lapping up my arousal cuts the air.

And I nearly fucking die.

My eyes roll back in my head as I flop onto my back.

"So fucking wet," he mutters, smacking his lips.

My cheeks heat because he's right. I'm dripping for him.

"So fucking good."

He draws my clit into his mouth and shoves two fingers into my channel and I cry out, my back lifting off the bed. Pressure builds in my core, tightens in my limbs, causes my body to tremor.

"Thatta girl," Cohen coos. "Come for me, baby. Show me how much you want my cock."

"Fuck," I cry.

Cohen's words coax as much of a reaction from my body as his touch.

He adds a third finger and pulses his tongue against the little ball of nerves.

I grind my pussy against his face. I'm close. So fucking close.

"Don't stop," I demand.

He curls his fingers in response and sucks hard on my clit.

I shatter. Break apart at the seams and swear wildly as the most intense pleasure of my life wracks through my veins. It's a tidal wave of rapture, flooding my senses with pure satisfaction. It's a release of epic proportions and I ride it.

Cohen helps by keeping his fingers inside me and pressing gentle kisses to my inner thighs.

"Holy shit," I wheeze, floating back to reality.

"You're gorgeous when you come," he says truthfully.

I drag my eyes open and stare down at him. He pulls his fingers out slowly and smears my want over my hips and up my stomach. Then, he laps it up like a dog and I fucking die.

His fingers caress my nipples, coating them with my arousal. He sucks them greedily.

"Cohen," I whimper. My body is wrung out. Even my flesh feels over-sensitive.

"So good, Rai," he murmurs.

I grab his face and pull his mouth to mine, kissing him deeply. I taste my want on his tongue, and it flips a switch, making me want him again.

I feel insatiable. All I want is Cohen Campbell.

His hard length jerks against my thigh.

"Get inside me, Cohen."

He chuckles, burying his face into my shoulder and biting my neck.

I widen my legs for him, trying to line us up.

"You want my cock, Rai?" He pulls back to look at me.

"Badly," I acknowledge.

I didn't think it was possible for Cohen to look more sinful, but his expression changes. The playful transforms into a hardness. A want so powerful, it's borderline possessive.

And I like it.

He sits back on his knees. Fists his cock. Pumps it slowly.

A bead of precum forms and his thumb brushes it away.

I watch in fascination, unable to blink.

"You want me to pound into you?" Cohen asks.

I rub my thighs together, wanting him to soothe the ache that's forming again. Will I ever get enough?

Probably not.

"Tell me," he demands.

"I want you to fuck me, Cohen. Hard. Relentlessly. Until I'm screaming your name," I admit, surprised by my honesty.

His eyes blow as he groans, pumping faster for two strokes.

"Fuck, you're gonna kill me. I love that my good girl has such a dirty mouth," he mutters, smacking the inside of my thigh. He reaches for his wallet on the nightstand and pulls out a condom, quickly rolling it on.

Then, he settles between my legs, lines us up, and holds my eyes. "Watch me take you, Rai. Watch how perfectly we fit. Don't you dare blink."

He pushes inside. Tantalizingly slow.

I watch, enraptured, as my body stretches to accommodate his length.

When he bottoms out, we both sigh in relief. Cohen presses into me, our chests rubbing against his each other's. His one hand holds my face, the other hooks behind my thigh. He kisses me once, hard and needy, and then he pulls out and drives back in.

"Oh, God, Cohen," I moan.

"That's it," he says, setting a pace that is the relentless I asked for. "That's my girl."

Cohen fucks me hard and fast. He swears through his release and collapses next to me. The bed dips as he discards the condom on the floor and reaches for a new one.

"What?" I pant as he rips open the wrapper.

Cohen grins at me wickedly. "Not done with you yet."

I've barely recovered from my second orgasm when he rolls on the fresh condom.

My eyes widen.

"You can take it," he murmurs, his hands caressing my hips. "Trust me."

I nod; I do.

Cohen enters me again and I wince at the twinge of soreness. Then, he kisses me sweetly, reverently, completely.

I relax under his touch, and he showers me with affection. Gentle hands and deep, soulful kisses.

"My beautiful love," he sighs. "You're pure perfection."

I mewl.

This time, he fucks me slowly. Thoroughly. And something changes.

Feelings I never experience blossom in my chest. My thighs quiver. My hands clutch at his biceps. I hold him flush against me. He cradles me into his frame.

We come together as one. Choosing and claiming. Acknowledging and accepting.

"My sweet Raia," Cohen sighs.

Our sex is more like lovemaking. Slow and steady. Deep and passionate.

We come on the same exhale, breathing in each other's words, our names a sigh on both our lips.

NINETEEN
COHEN

RAIA'S SLEEPING form greets me upon waking. What a hell of a way to wake up.

Her soft breathing is even and steady. Her dark hair is spread across her pillow. Her caramel highlights pop rich against the white bedding and I drag my fingertips over the smooth strands. Her mouth is adorable, puckered into a pout, and her eyelashes are long, sweeping over the crests of her cheeks.

Christ, she's gorgeous. I shift closer, my knees skimming over hers. She murmurs in her sleep and turns more fully into my frame, as if drawn to me with the same magnetism that pulls me closer to her.

Last night, we crossed the last line. The final barrier that will make it impossible for me to walk away. Saying goodbye will gut me on a level I don't want to consider.

It's not just the sex, it's the emotions that came with it. I made fucking love to her. After I fucked her hard.

What a mindfuck. What a perfect night.

Her eyes flutter open and the sweetest smile crosses her lips. "Good morning."

"It is," I agree, tugging her closer. I breathe her in, wishing I could shower in her scent. Keep her with me all damn day.

She comes willingly and presses a kiss to the center of my chest. "How'd you sleep?"

"I was out," I admit, wondering what time it is. "You broke my internal clock."

Raia giggles. Then, she sits up and glances out the window. "Whoa."

Turning, I take in the snow accumulating on the deck. Over a foot fell during the night and I imagine travel is going to be disastrous for the next few days.

Maybe we should have considered other options?

Maybe I should care more? Right now, the only thing on my mind is getting back inside of Raia.

My cock is hard and it's more than morning wood. It's needy for the woman who owned me—mind, body, and soul —just hours ago.

I shift uncomfortably and try to redirect my thoughts. "You think your friends are going to head out today?" I doubt they'll be able to access the airport.

"Probably not," she agrees, picking up her phone. Her eyes widen and snap to mine. "Cohen, it's two p.m."

"What?" I scoff. "No way." I swipe her phone from her hand and chuckle. "I can't remember the last time I slept in like this. We…"

"Were really exhausted last night," she says cheekily.

I smirk at my pretty girl. "You put me through calisthenics."

She chuckles. "Me? I could barely keep up with your insatiable appetite."

I reach for her, cup my hand around the back of her neck, and pull her in for a hard kiss. "You like my appetite."

She nips at my lower lip. "Like trying to keep up with you more." Her mouth curves into a smile. "I've never… Three times in one night is no joke."

I snort, liking that the douchebag who broke her heart never gave her as many orgasms in one go. That honor belongs to me. Damn straight it does.

I kiss her again and she pulls away, shaking her head at me. "We need to assess the situation. See what everyone is thinking." She slides from the bed.

Groaning because I'm not ready for this morning, this moment, to end, I reluctantly get up. It's not lost on me that I'm not as stressed as I should be. If we're snowed in, I'll be delayed getting back to Knoxville. I could miss a practice, or worse, a game.

No, that won't happen. I'll sort something out. Football has always been my top priority and I won't slack on my responsibilities or my commitment to my team.

But the fact that I'm not panicking about these possibilities is alarming in a different way. Raia's sashay over to the dresser distracts me and I inwardly swear.

I'm fully wrapped up in her. So much so, everything else in my life pales. She's the sun, blocking out my ability to see anything else clearly, and I don't care.

"Come on," she says, pulling on a hoodie. She slips her feet into fluffy slippers and leads the way toward the common area.

She stops short and I run into her back, wrapping an arm around her waist to keep her from toppling over. "Sorry," I mutter.

Raia doesn't respond. Instead, she looks around the picked-up, empty, and silent space. "They left."

"What?" I laugh. "No way. We would have heard them."

Raia turns and arches an eyebrow.

I chuckle. "Hang on." I walk deeper into the living room. "Beck? Faye? You guys here?"

Raia moves toward the kitchen island and picks up a piece of notebook paper. Waving it at me, she confirms, "They left."

"Seriously?"

Raia reads the note.

> *Hey! Y'all looked too peaceful to disturb. Plus, I think you will enjoy being snowed in in a way that we won't.*

"There's a smiley face with a sticking-out tongue here." Raia pauses to show me the caricature.

"Faye draws really well," I comment.

Raia snorts and continues to read.

> *Have fun. Be safe. Choose happiness. Love you, Faye and everyone else.*

I chuckle. "Everyone else?"

"She's clearly taking credit for the note."

"Clearly," I agree. Crossing my arms over my chest, I lean my ass against the lip of the kitchen counter and look at Raia. "What now?"

"Coffee?"

I grin. I love how easygoing she is. "Coffee," I confirm.

Raia brews a pot, and we settle into the afternoon. I make us bacon and eggs, grateful the refrigerator is stocked since there's no way we're going anywhere.

Raia flips on the television, and we learn that a blizzard pounded the area overnight, disrupting travel and effectively snowing us in.

"How long do you think?" I ask.

"A day, maybe two." She shrugs. Her eyebrows dip over her cloud gray eyes. "You worried about the team?"

I shake my head. "Not like I should be."

A slow smile crosses her face. She walks toward me, her long sweats dragging on the floor. Wrapping her arms around my waist, Raia leans back and stares at me. "You happy to be snowed in with me, Cohen?"

"Very happy, champ." I tap the tip of her nose. Then, I grab her ass and lift her up. Her legs encircle my waist, her arms snake behind my neck, and she lines our lips up. I give her a quick peck.

She grins. "Me too."

"Really?" I tease. "I never took you for a woman who would want to play house."

Her smile slips and I inwardly swear at myself. Am I making it too real when we have the opportunity to stay lost in this winter wonderland for a few more days? "It doesn't feel like we're playing anymore."

I let out a slow exhale. Her words make my heart rate jump. Does she feel the way I do? Does she want...more? "No, it doesn't."

I search her eyes and she stares back, giving me her uncertainty and confusion. She doesn't sugarcoat things. What you see is what you get. It's something I admire about her, but I'm also disappointed that she's not ready to dive in headfirst with me.

"The bacon's burning," she murmurs, disrupting the spell.

I let her slide down my frame so I can tend to the bacon. I plate our breakfast and we sit at the kitchen island together, eating in a comfortable silence.

"I'm going to text Avery to let him know what's going on," I say, pulling out my phone.

"Yeah. That's a good idea. I should check in with my mom and dad." She chews a bite of eggs. "After that, want to build a fire, play Uno, and day drink?"

I glance up, taken aback by her plans. Feeling my disappointment from moments ago fade as excitement thrums through my veins, I nod. "It's a plan, champ."

She drops her head, pushing her hair away from her face. "It's a date, Cohen."

I laugh, feeling relieved. "Okay, Rai."

Just because she's not ready to declare our relationship as real doesn't mean we're not finding our way there. Everything is different now. Last night, the way she moved, the way I held her, the moments we shared... It changed *everything*.

Deep down, we both know it.

I'm just willing to accept the inevitable before Raia is. I'm more comfortable with the leap we took. But fuck, I wish she was free-falling beside me, with her hand tucked into mine.

But it's okay, I reassure myself. We'll find our way into the future together. I need to be patient and understanding. This is scary and daunting for Raia. She just ended a decade-long relationship while I've been searching and biding my time for the right woman.

Now, I found her. I can't rush her. I have to be steady and compassionate. I have to show her that she can trust me. That I'm not going anywhere. That I'll always support her.

I need to be the man Raia needs, wants, and ultimately deserves.

TWENTY
RAIA

"ARE YOU SURE YOU'RE OKAY?" Mom asks for the third time.

"Mom! I'm fine," I promise.

Cohen is stoking the fire and I'm studying the perfect shape of his ass. Muscular thighs and tree-trunk legs. A tapered waist that widens into broad shoulders. The type of shoulders a girl can hang onto. The kind of strength that can carry the scars of a broken heart.

"Are you still there?" Mom asks.

"Huh? Yes, sorry." I shake my head.

"Everyone left?"

"Yep. Early this morning. But I'm with Cohen; I'm fine," I remind her.

"Well, that's true," she agrees, appeased.

I roll my eyes. My parents adore Cohen. That's a good thing, right? We'll be able to bypass the awkward meet-the-parents bit.

I mean, if we're dating for r   Are we?

"Just stay put, then. Thank   r calling, Raia; I was getting worried. I'm glad for you a   ohen. You could both use some time to recharge," Mom   inues.

"Thanks, Mom."

"Send me the details once you rebook your flight."

"I will."

"Okay. Stay safe, Rai."

"Bye, Mom." I end the call and toss my phone onto the couch.

Then I approach Cohen and wrap my arms around him from behind. Pressing my cheek into the center of his back, I give him a squeeze. His large hands skim over my forearms. He turns slowly, his arms automatically encircling my frame.

"Now we can do whatever we want," I announce.

Cohen laughs. "Yeah, that's true. Where do you want to start?" His fingertips tuck under the hem of my shirt and swipe over a path of my skin.

I bite my bottom lip. "I thought we could start with board games. Like Scrabble."

"Scrabble?" He arches an eyebrow. His fingers move higher.

"Yeah, you know, a smart game."

"Smart," he replies. The pads of his fingers glide over the underwire of my bra.

"Or Uno," I offer.

"Numbers," he replies. Now his palm is resting over my breast. His thumb swipes across my nipple. "I have a better idea."

"Oh?" I tip my chin up. My back arches slightly, pressing my breast more firmly in his hand.

"A much better idea," Cohen decides, pulling off my shirt. He discards it on the floor. Then, he slides the strap of my bra off my shoulder and bends to kiss the spot where my neck meets my shoulder.

"You could show me," I play along, my breathing accelerating.

"I could," he agrees, pushing my sweatpants off my hips.

I step out of them and kick them to the side. Then, I pull

down his basketball shorts. He loses his shirt. We stand in front of the fire in just our underwear.

"Where do you want to start?" I ask, trying to keep myself intact. To play along. To drag this out.

"Hmm." Cohen tilts his head, studying me. "Here," he decides, tracing my mouth with his thumb. "Then here." He runs his fingers between the valley of my breasts. "Then..." His hand cups my pussy.

I press myself into his hold and he smirks.

"How's that sound?" His voice is raspy.

"Perfect." I slide his boxers off his hips and drag them down his legs, lowering with them.

"Oh, fuck," he swears, staring down at me. I smile up at him. I'm already wet and wanting but Cohen, Cohen's hard as a rock. Scratch that. A boulder.

"My turn first," I remind him. Then, I fist his cock, and pull him in between my lips.

His fingers lace through my hair as he guides my head, setting the pace he likes.

I bob my head back and forth, taking him deeper.

Cohen swears. I close my eyes and imagine what we must look like, two insatiable lovers, snowed in at gorgeous ski chalet, in front of a blazing fire, with a blizzard raging outside.

It's as if someone turned a snow globe upside down but we're locked in the safety of the house, in the comfort of each other. And nothing else matters.

"You suck me so good," Cohen groans. He tugs me to stand up. "Don't want to come down your throat when I can finish inside you, baby."

Cohen tugs a thick, plaid blanket off the couch and lays me down on top of it. We stretch out in front of the fire. It warms our skin, and the crackling sounds of the logs create a cozy atmosphere.

When Cohen finally pushes inside me, I'm desperate. We

fuck on the floor. Then again in the shower. Once more on the kitchen island.

Cohen works me over so thoroughly, I can't form words. But it doesn't matter. Because we can read each other's wants. We give to each other freely and fully.

For the first time in months, I feel full. Whole. Loved.

I don't want to wake up from this fever dream. I don't want to go back to reality. I want to stay here, in this secret corner of the world, wrapped up in snowflakes, and fall deeper for Cohen Campbell.

"I can't believe we still have steaks," I say as I cut into the choice meat.

"I know." Cohen grins and clinks his wine glass against mine. "Lucky us."

"We are," I say, meaning it. Right now, I feel like the luckiest girl on the planet.

"Some ski trip," Cohen laughs. "I didn't ski, and you were out for about four hours."

I shrug. "This was the best ski trip I've ever been on."

"Me too." He takes a long pull of his wine, his eyes studying me over the rim. "It's cool you guys do this every year. When did it start?"

"Um, I think our sophomore year of high school. Preston's parents used to have a chalet in Aspen."

"Used to?"

I shrug. "Collateral damage in the divorce."

"Ah," Cohen comments. "I get the sense that none of your friends have great home lives."

"They're not bad," I say, a little defensively. "They never went without."

"Unless you count love," Cohen replies.

I dip my head in agreement. "Yeah. They didn't get affection or attention from their families the way they should have. Not like Anna and me."

"You feel better that you guys talked?" Cohen asks.

I nod, thinking over his question. "Yes, I do. There's some closure there but…"

"But?"

"I don't know if it will ever be the same between us. There's a trust factor that's been broken and I don't see how we can get it back. Our relationship will always be different now."

"Yeah," Cohen sighs. "That's shitty. I can't imagine how I'd feel if my brother, or your brother, betrayed my trust like that."

"The thing with Anna hurts more than breaking up with Brooks," I admit.

"Was it hard? Seeing him?" His voice is even but his eyes are intent on mine. Curious and wary.

"No. Not after the initial reaction. If I'm being honest…I think Brooks was right." I shake my head. "Don't fucking tell him."

"Never."

"But we did outgrow each other. I just couldn't see it. Or maybe I didn't want to admit it. I hate change, and this summer, well, everything is different now."

"It is," he agrees, his words heavy with another meaning.

I look at him, studying his expression.

"We have to tell Avery," he says.

I shove a bite of steak into my mouth and chew slowly, thinking.

What will my brother say? How will he react? Will this cause issues for the Coyotes?

"Raia," Cohen admonishes.

I sip a mouthful of wine.

"I won't lie to my best friend. Especially when what I feel for you… It's real."

"I know," I agree. "We need to handle it delicately. You have the team to think about."

Cohen's expression hardens for a second before he nods slowly. "I always put the team first."

"You should; they're a different kind of family."

Something that looks a lot like disappointment flickers across his face. It's gone too fast for me to confirm. "Yeah," he mumbles, polishing off his wine.

"We'll figure this out," I say, more for myself than him.

"I hope so," he replies, his tone hard.

I steer our conversation to lighter topics. We reminisce about our childhood and share stories from people in our hometown. He tells me more about the team this season, Gage's recovery from his ACL injury, and some details about the rookie, West.

I listen attentively, learning more about Cohen's life.

We enjoy another bottle of wine. He helps me clean up the kitchen. When I turn on a playlist, we dance around the space. Funky, ridiculous dance moves that give way to slow dancing in his arms.

When we fall asleep that night, I'm happy there's a blizzard. I'm relieved to have this time with Cohen. I revel in getting to know him, in lowering my guard and letting him in. I lay my ear on his chest and let the steady beat of his heart lull me to sleep.

I wish our wonderland was our reality.

Deep down, I know it's not. Nothing this good lasts. Nothing this perfect can be trusted.

I learned that firsthand by watching my friends' families cast them aside, by witnessing Avery break Mila's heart. By experiencing Brooks moving on with Anna.

If I allow myself to fall fully for Cohen, will he be there to catch me?

If I let him all the way in, will he eventually break my heart?

I hate that the word *yes* cuts through my head and twists in my chest.

"One more day," I beg Cohen.

He lifts an eyebrow. I toss a handful of chocolate chips in the pancakes I'm making.

"You really don't want to go home?" he asks.

"I like being here with you. Tucked away from the world."

"Yeah," he agrees, his eyes narrowing. "But this isn't our everyday lives…"

"It's better than reality," I refute. "Here, we can just be us."

"We can be us in Knoxville too," he reminds me.

I sigh and shrug.

"What?" Cohen asks, shifting closer.

"I just… I never feel at home there," I admit.

Surprise crosses his expression. "Because you haven't lived there in years?"

"No, even then…" I consider my words as I flip our pancakes. "When I'm in Knoxville, I feel…separate. Apart."

"From?" Cohen presses.

"Everyone. Everything," I huff, plating our pancakes. "You want whipped cream or maple syrup?"

"I got this." He takes the plates and sets them on the kitchen island. "I want to understand more about you not feeling at home in our hometown."

Internally, I kick myself for opening this can of worms. But, other than Anna and Mila, I've never admitted how I don't fit in in Knoxville. "It's Avery's city."

Cohen chuckles. When he realizes I'm serious, his mouth twists.

"He's the better Callaway," I continue. "The athlete. The golden boy. The Pride and Joy of Southern Football and the hometown hero."

"So?" Cohen asks, his eyes boring into mine.

"It just, it feels like there's not enough space for both of us. It's weird but if I try to…excel at something, soccer or school or whatever, it's as if I'm competing with him."

"But you're not," Cohen refutes. "You're competing with yourself."

"Everyone compares us all the time. Teachers and coaches and just, regular townspeople. I never fit in. By the time I was in high school, he'd already made a mark, a giant impression on everyone, and I always felt like I was failing at living up to the expectations he set."

"Raia," Cohen mutters. His tone is laced with surprise and concern, even a thread of anger.

"I'm not saying I'm right—"

"It's how you feel," he cuts me off.

I shrug. "Yeah. It's how I feel."

"I had no idea," he murmurs, as if to himself. "All these years, I never knew."

"It's not something I really talk about."

"Is that why you went away to boarding school?"

"Mostly, yes. But also, the soccer team there was exceptional, so it made sense on a practical level too. But it's why I don't ever want to live in Knoxville."

Cohen stops eating, his eyes snapping to mine. "You never want to live in Knoxville? Ever?"

I shake my head. "No plans to live in Tennessee. It's a place I like to visit from time to time, but I don't see myself there. Besides, I don't think you should ever go back. Not when you can keep moving forward."

Cohen's quiet as he considers my words. I shovel a mouthful of pancake into my mouth.

I wash it down with coffee and take a fortifying breath.

It feels like I just shattered some of our bliss. Chipped a bit of our idyllic snow globe by bringing in a slice of reality.

It was bound to happen eventually.

This weekend was going to come to an end.

I'm going to leave Tennessee.

And Cohen and I will go our separate ways.

That's always been the plan. Except the thought of those options tastes sour. Rancid.

And painful to swallow.

TWENTY-ONE
COHEN

"RAI, hey. It's time to wake up, sleepy." I give Raia a nudge.

She mumbles in her sleep, and I smile. She looks peaceful and innocent. Her sass is checked, and her expressive reactions are resting.

I run my thumb over her eyebrow, and she swats my hand away.

"She's awake," I joke.

Raia groans and opens one eye. It stares straight at me. "I don't want to leave."

Me neither. The last thing I want to do is board a plane and return to Knoxville. Not when the alternative is being tucked away with Raia, lost in each other.

"I know," I agree. "At least we got to enjoy our time here and didn't have to head out early like your friends."

"Whatever." She pouts, not in the mood for my positive outlook.

Her grumpiness causes my grin to widen. I slap her ass, grabbing one healthy cheek and give it an extra squeeze. "Move your body, babe. We don't want to miss our flight. I texted your brother last night and he's going to pick us up."

"'Kay," she mutters, closing her eye.

I chuckle and slide from the bed. While Raia takes her sweet time, I brew a pot of coffee, finish picking up the chalet, and ensure our bags are mostly packed.

When Raia enters the kitchen, dressed in baggy jeans, a cropped sweater, and boots, I pull a beanie on her head, kiss the tip of her nose, and press a to-go cup of coffee in her hand.

"You're the best," she breathes out.

I press a second kiss to her mouth. "This time with you was the best."

Her eyes flicker to mine. I note the uncertainty swimming in her gaze and wish she wanted this thing with me as much as I do. But Raia's always been honest and upfront about what this is—and isn't. I know better than to push her just because we obliterated the lines.

"Yeah," she says softly.

I dip my head and pull away. Heading into our bedroom, I grab her suitcase and load our rental car. I snap a quick photo of Raia, hanging on the front porch, gazing longingly at the mountains, her coffee in hand.

Man, I'm going to miss waking up to her each morning. Fucking her into slumber at night. This trip was a hell of a lot more than helping her save face. It was a game changer.

The way I feel about her, the things I want with her... I'm falling in love with my best friend's little sister. And I'm scared she doesn't feel the same way. That's not entirely true. I'm scared she won't let herself experience what could be with me.

A little twinge of doubt flickers in my chest and I rub the spot, as if that will extinguish the uncertainty.

"You ready?" she asks when she looks my way.

"Whenever you are."

Raia smirks and walks over to the car. She slides into the

passenger seat, I drop behind the steering wheel, and we set off for the airport. Now that the snow has been cleared and the blizzard has passed, it's time to re-enter our reality.

I hope it doesn't shatter the illusion of us. Because our fake relationship feels real. Our playing house filled me with yearning instead of terror. And the thought of kissing Raia goodbye for the last time haunts me.

"You ready to face off against Dallas?" she asks once we're on the highway.

I look at her. I have a game in three days, and I haven't thought about it once. Discomfort twists my stomach. "Uh, yeah," I mutter.

"Their QB has been on a roll lately," she adds, her hands doing half the talking. As Raia continues to fill me in on the backstory, a human-interest commentary, of Oliver Williams, I nod along.

But my thoughts splinter and spin in different directions.

Is she coming to the game?

Will she wear my jersey or Avery's?

How did I go three days without an intense workout?

How did I mentally block out the game against Dallas?

Will Mom and Dad be thrilled or appalled that I'm dating Raia?

Are we even dating? Or is this the beginning of the end?

Technically, we're supposed to break up before the Christmas holidays.

Thanksgiving is in a few days. Are we doing that together? Presenting a united front?

I glance at Raia. *How is she so cool? Normal?*

Does her heart not race like mine? Is she not agonizing over what comes next?

I shake my head and turn on my blinker to exit the highway.

"Here we go," Raia sighs as I pull into the car rental lane. She reaches over to touch my wrist. "Thanks for this week,

Cohen. I, God, I don't think I could have done it without you. I'm glad I didn't have to."

"Anytime, champ." I park our rental and turn to look at her.

She stares at me for a long beat, her eyes brimming with emotions she usually locks down. Before I can ask what's wrong, she leans over the center console, grips the back of my neck, and kisses me hard. She tastes like hazelnut and snowflakes. She feels like home.

"I owe you," she murmurs.

"It was my pleasure," I reply earnestly.

She arches an eyebrow, and we both laugh.

"I didn't mean it like that," I admit.

"Sure, you didn't," she scoffs.

Then, she slips from the car, and I force myself to stop checking out her ass. Instead, I settle up with the rental company, grab our luggage, and follow Raia to our terminal.

To our hometown.

Even though right now, it doesn't feel like home to me either.

We both zonk out during the flight. It passes quickly and before I realize it, our time together is officially over. We're waiting at baggage claim when I can't stand the uncertainty any longer.

"Rai," I sigh.

"I know." She steps closer to me.

I give her a look. "Know what?"

"We need to talk."

Jesus, thank you. "Yeah, we really do."

Raia slips her hand in mine, her eyes darting around the airport. "Now's not the time. Avery will be waiting outside.

But, this week with you, Cohen, it means something to me. Something more than fake."

Relief flows through me like an open faucet. I drag in a breath, feeling like I can inhale deeply for the first time in days. "Good. Me too. I am, fuck, Rai, it's all different now. I can't pretend this week didn't happen. I don't want to."

She grins, her eyes dancing. "Me neither."

I squeeze her fingers. "Where do we go from here?"

"I'm not sure," she admits. "But I want to figure it out. I think we owe it to ourselves, to each other, to see...what could be between us."

"Hell yeah, we do." I nod. "We gotta sit down and talk though. Work through things."

"I know."

"Before Thanksgiving," I tack on. I don't want this shit hanging over my head during the holiday, during our game against Dallas, during the rest of the damn week.

"We will," she promises, shuffling closer. She looks up at me and smiles. Her gray eyes shimmer and her expression is filled with an affection that's warmer than any hug. "Thank you again, Cohen. What you did for me..."

"It was nothing."

"It was everything." She presses up onto her tippy toes.

"Ah, champ." I drop her hand to sling an arm around her waist. Then, I kiss her, pouring everything I hope we'll be down her throat like a shot of tequila. It's a quick and dirty kiss, given our surroundings. But still, hot as hell, and I wish we had more time.

Just, more.

When Raia pulls back, she rolls her lips together and suppresses a giggle. "I could get lost in you, Cohen."

"You say it like it's a bad thing."

Raia shakes her head but she's grinning. "There's my suitcase." She points to the carousel.

I swipe our luggage off the belt, and we turn toward the

exit. As soon as we step outside, I note Avery's truck. He's staring at us through the windshield, his expression tight. His fingers drum on top of the steering wheel.

"Damn, what do you think crawled up his ass?" Raia asks.

I shrug. "Bad date?"

She snorts. "My brother doesn't waste his time on *dates*."

I let that go, knowing that for as much love as there is between the Callaway siblings, there's also an undercurrent of competition and pain. Something I'm only just beginning to recognize.

Now that Raia confided in me, I see how difficult it would be to grow up in Avery's shadow. Hell, sometimes it's tough to be his best friend.

I roll our suitcases around to slide them into the bed of the truck.

Raia jumps into the passenger seat, and I slip into the back. Avery meets my gaze in the rearview mirror. His jaw is tight, his eyes hard.

"Hey! All good?" I ask.

He pulls away from the curb and eases into the traffic.

"You tell me," he replies, his tone clipped.

I jerk back, surprised by the coldness in his voice.

Raia rolls her eyes. "The trip was great, thanks for asking. Cohen totally pulled it off."

Avery snorts.

"Everyone bought it," Raia continues. "I think Beck tried to initiate a bromance with Cohen, too."

Avery grins for real at that comment.

"So, it was a good week?" Avery asks, merging onto the highway.

"A great week," Raia confirms.

My best friend nods. His eyes flick to me in the back seat before turning toward his sister. "And is your fake relationship over now that your mission is accomplished? Or are you guys seriously dating?"

Fuck. I straighten in my seat.

Did one of Raia's friends tell him we slept together?

Did he see a photo from the weekend?

Did he catch on by how many of his calls I avoided answering?

"Because the way y'all fucking kissed in the airport looked a lot more than a friend helping out a friend."

Ah, shit. The airport kiss.

TWENTY-TWO
RAIA

MY HEART LURCHES into my throat and my stomach twists.

Avery looks...hurt. Disappointed. And yeah, there's definitely a bite of anger to his tone but it's not the emotion he's leading with.

"Look, man," Cohen says from the back seat. He shifts forward, placing a hand on Avery's seat and leaning over the center console. "You know—"

"I can't believe you bought it, too!" I exclaim, the words bursting from the pit of my stomach and exploding in the tense car like a stick of dynamite.

Avery and Cohen's eyes swing in my direction. But I can't meet either of their gazes. Instead, I try to block out the hurt emanating from Cohen's expression. I avoid meeting my brother's disappointment.

And I lie through my fucking teeth, my eyes trained on a spot above Avery's ear.

"It's like method acting," I continue, babbling. "We did such a great job this trip. We were such a great *team*," I gush. "We just...got caught up in it for a second. I guess. Right?" I turn toward Cohen and stare at his top lip.

Even though I avoid eye contact, it would be impossible to miss the frustration blazing in his eyes. Can't unsee the hurt in the lines of his face. Can't pretend his lips aren't twisted in a grimace.

Avery glances in the rearview mirror.

Cohen clears his throat. "Yeah. Trip was solid. Your sister definitely saved face," Cohen backs me up. Except his voice is monotone. His features flat.

I feel him disengage. The space between us shivers with a detachment that annoys me. The aloofness that seeps from his demeanor scrapes and the worst part is—I deserve it.

Hell, I fucking caused it.

Avery grunts and his shoulders drop. "Fuck, y'all scared me for a second there. The way you looked at each other…" He shakes his head. Glances at me. "You sure it's all good?"

I beam. My cheeks ache. "All good. Great, even."

Cohen slides back and shifts over to the window, looking at the passing scenery.

Avery nods.

I reach forward and turn on some music. Anything to drown out the new tension emanating in the vehicle. Something to focus on other than how I just lied to my brother and hurt Cohen in the process.

But what did he expect me to say?

That I've fallen in love with him?

That I'm second-guessing my way forward with soccer because I hate the thought of leaving him?

That these past few weeks have flipped my world upside down and affected me deeper than Brooks's breakup did?

I know Cohen's been wanting to talk about…us. But I thought we had more time. I didn't anticipate Avery putting us on blast. I let my nerves rule my response and, in the process, hurt the guy I've fallen for.

When Avery pulls in front of Cohen's condo building, shame

burns through me. I can barely look at him as guilt swirls in my stomach. My heartbeat thrums in my temples and Avery's voice sounds faraway as he tells Cohen he'll call him later.

"Yep. Later," Cohen tosses over his shoulder before closing the truck door. He grabs his suitcase and enters his condo building without a backward glance.

Relief and horror war for space in my mind. I sink in my seat as ice blasts through my veins.

Shit. I messed this up.

My throat tightens and my nose burns. I blink rapidly and let out a slow exhale, locking down my emotions until I'm home, in the safety of my bedroom.

Avery sighs and pulls out of the parking lot.

"Thanks for picking us up," I mutter, clearing my throat.

"No problem," Avery replies, glancing at me. He swears. "Rai, is all cool with you and Cohen?"

I swipe my fingers over my eyes, as if wiping away exhaustion instead of regret. "What? Yeah. Why?"

He shakes his head. "That was fucking weird."

I dip my head in agreement.

"Cohen's not usually so…"

"Awkward," I supply, internally cringing. Why am I making this worse? Why can't I tell Avery that I like his best friend? That I more than like him.

Avery will understand, eventually. I think. And it doesn't matter what he thinks anyway. I'm an adult. I've spent the past decade trying to prove that I don't need to live up to Avery's expectations. I don't need to prove anything to anyone, except myself.

The thought causes me to sit up straighter and turn toward my brother. I open my mouth…and close it. The truth doesn't tumble out. Nothing does.

"Affected," Avery replies.

I wince and turn away.

"Look, he's been my best friend for years," my brother continues.

My shoulders roll forward as I curl into myself. Now he's going to tell me that I shouldn't jeopardize his friendship. Or that Cohen's a player and not into monogamous commitment, like I am.

"He holds himself back until he's all in. But once he is, it's permanent, Rai. Cohen doesn't do anything by degrees. He's all or nothing."

I make a nonsensical sound in my throat. My eyes sting and I widen them, hoping to keep my tears from forming. Or worse, falling.

"You're leaving," he reminds me.

"It was just a ski trip." I sound defensive. Hell, I *am* defensive.

"And you earned the chance to have your shot at your dream career," Avery continues. "You worked your ass off for this. I don't want either of you to have regrets."

"He helped me out. That's all," I double down, a lump in my throat. He's worried about...both of us! I didn't see that coming. In fact, Avery's understanding makes me feel worse.

Oh God, I screwed up. Badly.

Avery shrugs and turns into our parents' driveway. "All right. Good. That makes things easier." He smirks. "Glad it worked out for you this weekend and you got a break from Mom and Dad's, too."

"Yeah," I murmur. "A break from the whole town."

My brother's brow furrows. "What do you mean?"

I sigh and shake my head. I didn't think it was possible to feel worse. "Nothing. Thanks for the lift, Ave."

"Yeah," he agrees, looking confused. "I'll grab your suitcase and head in."

"'Kay," I agree, slipping from his truck.

I dash up the front steps and into Mom and Dad's.

I beeline for the bathroom, closing the door and stealing a

few moments to pull myself together. I can barely tolerate my reflection in the mirror.

I lied to Avery.

Fuck. I lied to myself.

And in the process, I *hurt* Cohen.

Ashamed, I turn away and force myself to go through the motions. Unpacking my suitcase, starting a load of laundry, filling Mom and Dad in about the trip...

That night, we sit around the kitchen table and have a family dinner. There's a slice of normalcy to it. A nostalgia that bowls me over. I miss it; I miss this. My family.

Again, it hits me how long I've been away. How long I stayed away, thinking I didn't belong. But Mom, Dad, and Avery pull me into conversation and smile at me. They say how nice it is to have me home. How much they missed me.

They break a piece of my heart.

The rest of it is crushed by Cohen. By how I treated Cohen. I'm furious with myself and desperate to apologize to him. To make amends.

But Cohen avoids my calls and messages for the remainder of the night.

I don't blame him; I deserve his silence.

RAIA

Hey! Sorry about earlier. Call me?

Did you crash for the night, or are you avoiding me?

I wouldn't blame you for avoiding me, but we should talk...

Are you working out tomorrow morning?

Cohen, I'm sorry. Really sorry.

The next morning, I'm at the Coyotes training facility early. I don't want to miss running into Cohen since he's clearly avoiding me. Waking up without a return message from him hit me like a sucker punch, proving how badly I screwed this up.

We need to clear the air. I've had to do that too many times the past few months, which indicates that I'm a shitty communicator in my relationships.

I swear when I enter the gym and note Gutierrez and Jag working out.

"Ah, here she is," Gage calls out, slow clapping.

"Thought you blew us off. You went skiing?" Jag asks. "You must be feeling good as new."

I chuckle. "Not too bad," I agree.

"Yo, way to get our boy to go with you! That's fucking... big," Gage tacks on.

"Yep," Jag agrees. "Cohen doesn't go out of his way like that for anyone."

"He barely dates anyone long enough to make it to a 'meet-the-friends stage,'" Gage muses.

Jag hits him in the stomach with the back of his hand.

"Sorry," Gage croaks.

I shrug.

"Shit's different with you, Rai," Jag says. "We all see it. And Cohen, he looks happier, too."

"We're happy for y'all," Gage admits.

"Thanks, guys!" I force myself to act normal and open my arms to give them a group hug. "It's nice to come home and feel welcomed."

"Huh?" Gage pulls back. "You're always welcome here, Rai. You know that."

"You're an honorary Coyote," Jag agrees.

I manage a laugh and shake my head. Has it always been like this? Have these guys embraced me, and I pushed them away? Have I been running from...nothing? Or worse, myself?

The thought loops in my mind when I see Cohen push into the gym.

My mouth dries at the sight of him. God, he rocks sweats like no man I've ever seen. But my heart twists too. Because he looks as miserable as I feel.

"Hey!" I call out, walking toward him.

"Yo," he replies, his expression blank.

I snort. "Seriously?"

"What?"

"You're going to play it like this?" My shame simmers but my anger spikes.

He shrugs. "We're cool, right? Wasn't this your idea? We do the trip and go our separate ways."

"Cohen, stop. I'm sorry, okay?" My voice breaks and a sliver of compassion cuts through his eyes. "Please, just, talk to me." I grab his arm and pull him out of the gym and into a hallway.

"What are you doing?"

"We should clear the air."

He snorts.

"I want to talk to you. About...this."

"But not us?" His voice is quiet. Growly.

I swear and pull open a door. It's a supply closet but right now, I don't care. It's empty, lit up, and no one will walk in on us.

I push Cohen inside and close the door.

He leans against a rack of folded towels and crosses his arms over his chest.

"Look, I'm sorry," I repeat.

"About which part?" He tilts his head.

"What?"

Cohen stands straighter, his large frame towering over me. "About which part, Rai? Are you sorry for making me think things between us meant more than they do? Are you sorry for forcing my hand, and making me lie to my best fucking friend when I swore to be honest with him? Are you sorry for getting under my skin and twisting me up? Or—"

"All of it!" I exclaim, throwing my hands in the air. "I'm sorry for all of it, Cohen." Pent-up frustration, mostly with myself, gathers in my palms. I slap my hands on his chest and give him a little shove. "The way I feel about you, it's…"

"What?" he demands, grasping my wrists.

"It's overwhelming," I admit. "And maddening." I step into him. "It's everything I never knew it could be…" I break off, my eyes latching onto his.

My fingers curl into his shirt.

We're both breathing heavily, our bodies coiled with tension that has nowhere to go.

Before I can finish my thought, Cohen snaps. My hands are glued to his pecs and his mouth is on mine. He kisses me hard, with an edge. He's pissed and he shows it by how he steps into me, erasing all the space between us and dragging me into a vortex of heady emotions and complicated feelings.

Cohen sucks my tongue and I scrape at his chest, shoving him back into the towel rack. His shoulder blades rattle the metal. He shoots me a wolfish grin before whipping my tank and sports bra over my head. He snaps the clothing against my hip before dropping it on the floor. As he tugs off his shirt, my hands are already in the waistband of his shorts, shoving them down his hips until his cock springs free.

"You're already hard for me," I bite out, my tone accusing.

"Always fucking hard for you," he growls. "You drive me crazy."

I fist his length and he hisses.

"I fucked up and I'm sorry," I admit, my tone harsh. "But don't cut me out. Don't ignore me."

He swears colorfully. "Ignore you?" He chuckles but the sound is jarring. "I want you all the goddamn time." Cohen shuffles back half a step, his arm knocking a stack of orange cones off a shelf. They clatter to the floor, break apart, and roll by our feet.

We ignore them. Cohen swats my hand away and drops to his knees. Wrapping his arms around me, he pulls me into his frame, his mouth on my breast, one hand diving underneath my leggings and playing in between my legs.

The sound of my arousal can be heard over my panting. I'm slick with need, wild with want.

"Gonna make you come so many goddamn times," Cohen promises. Then, he rakes my leggings down to my knees, drags his tongue up my core two times, and stands. He gathers me with him, my legs wrapping around his waist, my nails scoring the skin on his strong back.

He turns us fiercely, pinning me up against the shelving unit. The metal is cold on my bare skin, but I don't care. All I want is Cohen. For Cohen to get inside me.

"Condom," he huffs.

I shake my head. "I don't care."

"What?" He pulls back, his eyes unfocused as they latch onto mine.

"Get in me. Now!" I demand. "I'm on the pill."

That's all he needs to hear before he drives into me, bottoming out in one sharp thrust.

We both groan. I drop my head back. Gripping onto one of the shelf rails, I hold tight as more items clatter to the floor.

I'm vaguely aware that we're being loud as hell, but I dismiss it. It doesn't matter. In this moment, nothing matters except Cohen. His forgiveness. His touch. Our joining.

The gathering pleasure forming in my center. The desperate need to release.

My thighs quake as he continues to drive into me. His pace is relentless. The tendons in his neck are on full display. A gleam of sweat coats his chest. With wild eyes, flaring nostrils, and bulging biceps, Cohen fucks me like an animal unleashed. Like I'm both sin and salvation and he can't get enough. The moment stretches between us like a rubber band, taut enough to snap. He smacks my ass and I squeal, the sting more pleasure than pain.

I'm hanging onto both railings now, cursing Cohen. "Harder," I command.

"Gonna give it you," he swears through gritted teeth.

"I want it."

"Fuck. Want you."

"I'm gonna come," I cry out, my eyes nearly rolling back in my head.

"Come for me, Rai. Wanna see you fucking shatter."

I do. I break apart like an asteroid falling out of orbit. My body detonates. My thoughts scatter. Blinding light envelops me as pleasure—intense, powerful, and all-consuming—shoots through my limbs, hollows out my stomach, and floods my chest.

"Oh, fuck, Rai. Fuck, baby," Cohen cries out as he spills inside me.

"Cohen," I pant, holding him close. Our chests slide across each other, slick with sweat.

"Got you," he promises, his hand splayed in the center of my back.

"Jesus," I murmur, as I nearly collapse. My legs are jelly and if they weren't wrapped around Cohen, I'd face-plant.

Our eyes connect for one exhale. I note the disbelief in his expression. He's just as affected by our exchange as me. It was otherworldly. Like nothing I've ever experienced. Something I can't put into words.

I open my mouth and—the door swings open.

"Oh, fuck!" Avery swears, averting his gaze.

"Damn, Cohen," Jag laughs, his eyes widening.

"Close the door!" Cohen yells, turning so his ass is on full display and I'm shielded as much as possible by his large frame.

"Gladly," Gage snorts. The door slams shut.

"Fuck," Cohen whispers, lowering me.

He slips out of me and a rush of his cum coats my inner thighs. He swears, barely looking at me, as he tosses me his T-shirt. "Use this to clean up."

I do, destroying his shirt. My fingers tremble as I curl them into the cotton. A lump forms in my throat and tears burn the backs of my eyes. My body is a mess of emotions, my mind a tangled web of half-truths.

Cohen dresses quickly and turns away, giving me privacy. I feel the loss of his attention acutely. It's as if I was basking in sunshine and now, I'm surrounded by shadows.

The heat in the small space has plummeted to an arctic chill.

I shiver and dress on autopilot. I stare at the back of Cohen's head. His shoulder blades are bunched with tension. His breathing is even, but he swears softly to himself.

He reaches for the doorknob and pauses. Glancing back, he asks, "You good?"

I nod, my eyes trained on the door. "Fine."

I feel his gaze on my cheek but this time, I don't meet his eyes.

Cohen opens the door.

Avery leans against the opposite wall. His expression is murderous. His arms are crossed over his chest, and he can barely look at me.

"It was just a friend helping a friend, huh?" he accuses.

Beside me, Cohen's body locks down. And I wonder if I just lost my brother and the man I'm in love with.

TWENTY-THREE
COHEN

"AVE, IT'S COMPLICATED," I start, stepping toward my best friend.

He pushes off the wall and grabs the base of my neck. I'm shirtless, since I tossed Raia my T-shirt to use. Avery's fingers dig into my neck, and I let him. He should get a good jab in. He fucking deserves to deck me for the way I just fucked his sister in a goddamn supply closet.

Christ, we were loud. Rough. Furious.

"Fuck you," my best friend spits. His fingers flex on my neck before he shoves me away. "I can't even look at you guys. How could you—"

"Avery, I'm an adult," Raia throws out.

Avery shakes his head. "How could you lie to me?" He glares at me. He looks disgusted. Betrayed. Fucking hurt. "You fucking lied. After all the shit we've been through. Seriously, Cohen?"

"Ave, I'm—" I start.

But he cuts me off. "No, I don't want to hear it. I don't have time for this shit right now. We're playing Dallas this week." With that, he stalks off toward the gym. He presses against the double doors so hard, they bang off the walls, and close with a snap.

"He was my ride here," Raia mutters softly.

I close my eyes. Try to calm the adrenaline racing through my veins. Get a handle on the thoughts buzzing in my eardrums.

"I'll take you home," I say, moving toward the exit.

Raia follows without a word.

Silence stretches between us as I pull out of the parking lot and drive toward her parents' house.

"We should talk," she says quietly.

"Yeah."

I feel her look at me, study my profile, but I keep my eyes glued to the road. My grip tightens on the steering wheel.

These next few moments will be telling. My heartbeat thuds in my temples. This is it. It all comes down to now.

I've never felt more on edge. Not even during the play-offs, in the fourth quarter, when we were down three points with forty-two seconds on the clock.

That game, the restlessness that crawled up my spine, the energy that skittered in my palms, paled in comparison to this moment.

What is Raia going to say? What the hell does she want from me?

Did I just ruin a twenty-five-plus year friendship and my bond with my team for a woman who is going to cut me loose?

"What do you want, champ?" I ask, my voice chillier than I intend.

"I don't know what I'm doing with you, Cohen." Her voice is small.

Ouch, that fucking hurt. As if a physical blow, my hand rubs against the center of my chest. The pressure there doesn't alleviate.

"I didn't mean it like..." Raia trails off. She collects her thoughts and sighs. "That was...incredible. You're incredible, Cohen."

I glance at her, try to gage her expression. *Where is she going with this?*

"I don't know what anything means between us. I feel out of my element, trying to navigate everything I feel for you. Cohen, they're big. My feelings."

I soften slightly as she struggles to explain herself. "So, talk to me, Rai. Like a person. Like a *friend*," I remind her. "Don't give me mixed signals. I hate that shit. I'm an upfront guy, Raia. You know that about me; you've always known that about me."

"You're right."

"So, what gives? What do you want?"

She shakes her head. "I don't know. I don't know where we go from here," she admits. "The way I feel about you it's...it's overwhelming, Cohen. My future is a big question mark. I just got out of a decade-long relationship. And I don't want to ruin things between us. Or between you and Avery. Or the team."

I snort. "A little late for that, don't you think, babe?"

She rears back at the snark in my tone. But I'm past caring.

Because I feel like I just got taken down by a linebacker. Breath squeezes from my lungs. My limbs feel like deadweight. My mind blanks.

I give her one last shot. Push in all my chips. Take the Hail Mary.

"I want you, Raia." My voice is low. "I want all of you. I don't want to lie to my best friend. I don't want to keep shit from my team. I don't want to fake date you or trick the town or play fucking games. I want to be your man. But I don't settle. Never fucking have. And I'm not willing to keep putting myself out there for you to jerk me around. It's obvious you're not ready for this." I point between us. "And that's okay. But I don't want to keep doing this half-in, half-out thing either."

Raia sucks in an inhale. "So, that's it? You're calling it?"

I glance at her. "Didn't you already call it when you lied to Avery? When you dragged me into a utility closet? When you keep pretending this is fake when it's the realest fucking thing I've ever done?"

Raia rears back. I count to five in my head, waiting for her to refute my words. Waiting for her to say something.

Say something, dammit!

But she's silent. The quiet hovers between us, a barrier as we both throw up our defense mechanisms. I pull next to the curb in front of her parents' house.

"Cohen, I —"

"Take care of yourself, Rai," I cut her off. I don't want to hear any more of her apologies.

She shakes her head, her eyes wide. "That's it?" Her voice breaks.

I shrug. "Guess so."

Tears fill her eyes. "I'm sorry, Cohen. I never meant to hurt you."

"I know. I never meant for this to...become what it is."

"Yeah," she whispers.

We both skirt around the elephant taking up all the space, all the oxygen, in the SUV.

Raia gives me one last searching look. Then, she exits my ride, and races up the front walk. She disappears inside her house, closing the front door without a backward glance.

I sit out front for five minutes, hoping and praying she'll come back. That she'll admit she made a mistake. She'll say she wants to give us a real chance. That she's fallen for me, too.

She doesn't. Instead, the curtains in the upstairs window flutter and I catch a glimpse of Mrs. C. Her expression is filled with understanding. Compassion. Maybe even pity.

That's my cue.

I pull away from the curb and drive back to the Coyotes facilities. By the time I arrive, I pray most of the guys are done with their workouts. I pop in AirPods, crank up the volume, and commit to a heavy workout.

I feel raw and exposed. Confused and hurt.

But also relieved because I know Raia won't be here.

Her sweet curves and tight body won't distract me.

Her sassy jokes and airy laugh won't make me smile.

It'll just be me and the weights.

Focus, commitment, discipline.

Back to football. The one thing that never lets me down.

"WHAT HAPPENED?" Mom's voice is soft as she enters my bedroom.

I'm lying face down on my bed, sobbing into my pillow.

"Oh, honey." Mom sits on the edge of my bed. Her hand passes over my hair, stroking it the way she did when I was a little girl and couldn't fall asleep.

For some reason, the sweet gesture causes me to cry harder.

Mom lets me cry it out. She sits with me in silence for a long stretch, until there are no more tears. Until my eyes feel puffy and my heart rate slows.

I pull myself into a seated position, wipe my hands over my face, and meet her eyes. "We broke up."

"I'm so sorry, Raia. I really thought—"

"It was all fake," I admit, coming clean.

Mom frowns.

I squeeze my eyes shut and release an exhale. Then, I meet Mom's confused gaze and tell her the truth. "I begged Cohen to be my fake boyfriend so I wouldn't have to go on the ski trip solo. I didn't want to see Brooks and Anna together.

Cohen agreed but somewhere along the way...I fell in love with him, Mom."

Mom's expression morphs from surprise to understanding to empathy. She holds my hand and grips it lightly. "He doesn't feel the same way?"

I shake my head.

"Oh, Rai. The way—"

"No," I interject. "I didn't tell him how I feel. When he pushed for an answer, a commitment, I chickened out. I was going to tell him the truth today but then we... and Avery... and I, I hurt Cohen, Mom. You know what? It's so much worse than being the person in the relationship who gets hurt." Now that I've experienced both, the dumpee and the dumper, I'd rather be broken up with than cause someone else this kind of heartache.

"Raia, you are one of the most independent, fearless, determined women I've ever known."

I look up in surprise.

Mom smiles gently. "You were a pain in the ass to raise."

I snort, dragging a hand over my face to wipe my tears.

"But you never failed to amaze me with the things you've accomplished. You don't have to choose—Cohen or soccer. Tennessee or Spain. You can have both. You can figure it out. You just have to trust yourself."

I frown. "Do you really think so?"

"Yes. Your heart knows what it wants. Don't let it be at odds with your head. Let them work together. If anyone can juggle and balance things, it's you, Rai. I've watched you grow up and blossom into a fearless woman."

I shake my head. Wipe the snot from my nose.

Mom reaches over and plucks a tissue from my nightstand. She passes it to me.

"Thanks," I mutter.

"Don't give up on yourself. If you want soccer, fight for it.

If you want Cohen, fight for him. You, my darling, beautiful girl, can have both. You can have it all."

I stare at my mom, realizing how many heart-to-hearts and pep talks I've missed out on by not calling. Or visiting.

She opens her arms and I fall into them. I sigh in relief and let my body fall slack, trusting that my mom will hold me together.

She does. Mom wraps me in a tight hug and kisses my temple.

"I know I shouldn't say this but I'm happy you let Anna and Brooks think you moved on. I mean, it's true since you're this upset over Cohen. But I understand why you wanted to save face. You've been through a lot these past few months."

I pull back and give Mom a look. "Really? I thought you'd be upset I lied or—"

Mom shakes her head. "When I was your age, I would have keyed his car and stolen her favorite leather jacket."

"Mom!"

Mom chuckles, her eyes glittering. "Where do you think you get your independent streak from?"

I shake my head. It's another thing I never thought about.

Mom grins. "The apple doesn't fall far from the tree, Rai. I know this is the last place you wanted to be this summer, but I'm glad you're home."

I give her another hug. "It's not the *last* place."

Mom raises an eyebrow. I roll my eyes.

Mom chuckles, I laugh, and then, we crack up together.

When our laughter subsides, I pull myself together. I feel emotionally drained and lighter than I have in years. "You think Cohen will forgive me?"

"Only one way to find out." Mom passes me my phone.

She leaves me alone and I hear her exclaim a greeting to Avery.

I debate if I should call or text Cohen. Will he respond?

Before I make up my mind, my brother knocks on my bedroom door.

I drop my phone and face Avery, embarrassment flooding my cheeks.

"I know you're angry—" I start to explain but he cuts me off.

"Yeah. You know why?"

I frown. Scooting back on my bed, I pull my knees into my chest and recline against my headboard. Avery sits at the foot of my bed, watching me closely. "Because I'm kind of dating your best friend?"

He snorts and shakes his head. "Because you lied to me, Rai. You lied to my face."

"I'm sorry."

"Me too," he admits, narrowing his eyes. "It bothers me that you don't trust me enough to be honest."

I arch an eyebrow. "Are you seriously pretending like you wouldn't be mad that Cohen and I are...you know?"

"I'm not pretending. If you guys talked to me and were honest, yeah, I'd have some reservations. Like, are you sure you're ready to jump into something new when you just got out of a decade-long relationship? Or are you and Cohen being upfront that you've only had one serious relationship and he's had none? Or do you both want the same things? Have you considered long-distance when you move to Spain? Are you still moving to Spain?" He rattles off questions at a rapid pace.

I hold up a hand. "See? You're spinning."

"I'm not." He shakes his head. "I'd have reservations, Rai, because you and Cohen are two of the most important people in my life and I wouldn't want either of you to get hurt."

"Well, too fucking late," I grumble. "I already hurt Cohen."

"Yeah," Avery agrees. "And now you're hurting too."

I lift my gaze to his and heave out a sigh. "Why are you being so understanding about this?"

Avery smirks. "You're my sister, Raia. And you never come home. I want you to want to be here. In this town, this house…" He snorts. "In this family."

I look away, feeling my cheeks flame. "Me too."

"So be here. And be honest. I'm your brother. I'll always have your back and choose your side."

I look at him again. The sincerity in his expression makes me feel worse. "I've fallen in love with Cohen."

"No shit."

I gasp and Avery swears.

"I need to attend therapy from catching y'all in a goddamn supply closet," he adds.

I laugh, clapping a hand over my mouth. "That was intense and—"

"Don't talk about it," Avery groans. "Just, be honest with yourself. And Cohen. And me, Raia. Be the badass I know you are and decide what you want. Then, chase that shit down and don't let anyone stand in your way."

I shift onto my knees and lunge for my brother. He catches me easily, the way he did when I was a kid. We hug for a long moment, and I try to remember the last time we hugged like this.

I can't and that makes me sad.

"I'm sorry, Avery," I murmur, apologizing for so much more than today. And the supply closet.

He kisses my cheek and gives me a squeeze. "Me too, Rai. But I'm happy you're home."

I pull back and glance at him. "So am I."

"Avery! Raia! It's dinnertime," Mom's voice floats up the stairs.

My brother and I smile. "Like old times, yeah?"

I slide off my bed and dart for the stairs. "Yeah! Last one down has to wash the dishes."

I hear him clamber behind me but know he won't catch up. I'm already sliding down the banister.

"She beat you!" Dad bellows as I clear the landing.

"Such a pain in the ass," Avery grumbles.

Dad chuckles. "I'll let you have a beer as a consolation prize," he tells Avery, winking at me. I wink back.

As I turn into the kitchen, Mom's face is beaming. She looks at me with pure love shimmering in her gaze. I smile back and finally feel like I belong. Like I'm home.

I sit around the dinner table with my family. There's nothing particularly special about it. Except it's everything I thought I didn't need, but truly want.

TWENTY-FIVE
COHEN

"HOW BAD IS IT?" Coop asks. He drops into the chair beside me on his front porch and I pass him a beer from the six-pack I brought over. While my brother was still at work, I made myself at home, and spent the past hour hanging on his porch, watching dusk settle.

I glance at him, and he pops the tab at my response.

Cooper sighs and we sit in silence, looking over his quiet, peaceful street. While I live in the bustle of the city, Cooper prefers the stillness of the country. Right now, I need a slice of his haven to quiet my thoughts.

"Is she hurting as badly as you?" he asks.

"Maybe even more," I admit.

"Who wanted it more? Who laid everything on the line first?" Coop fishes.

I chortle bitterly. "Does it matter?"

"Ah," he murmurs. "You leaped; she faltered."

"Something like that." I take a swig of my second beer.

Cooper's quiet. Several fireflies flicker on and off in his front yard.

"You think she's scared?" he murmurs quietly.

I close my eyes and swear. "Yeah. That's exactly what I think."

"Maybe she needs more time."

"Maybe."

Cooper chuckles. I turn to glare at him. "What?" I ask.

"Nothing." My brother shakes his head.

"Why are you laughing?" I press.

"Isn't it kind of ironic? Cohen, do you realize how many women have leapt for you while you faltered? How many women wanted the reassurances and the promises and the answers while you waffled? And yeah, maybe it was because your heart wasn't in it. But do you think that of Raia? Do you think she's not sure about you? Or not sure about anything? Because those aren't the same things and she's been through a lot in a short amount of time."

I cluck a nonsensical sound and take a long pull of my beer. I hate that Coop has a point. I don't want his logic. I want him to sympathize with me. Right now, I feel lower than I have in years. My stomach is knotted, my head pounds, and frustration has every cell in my body tightening. I'm stressed and angry. Hurt and disappointed. Emotional when I strive for rational.

"Give her time," Coop advises.

I swing my eyes to his. "I did. This has been going on for weeks, Coop. There've been a lot of opportunities for her to commit. To confess. To fucking confide in me. Guess what? She didn't take any of them."

"Yeah?" He lifts an eyebrow. "Was she supposed to do that while preparing to face her ex-boyfriend and cousin? Or while she was in the same house with them and had all her friends as witnesses? This is little Raia Callaway we're talking about. That girl does not like to make herself vulnerable. She holds her cards close to the chest; she always has. She's not going to spill her guts because you asked her to."

My phone buzzes with an incoming message and I pull it from my pocket.

AVERY:

Come for Thanksgiving dinner.

"Seriously?" I mutter.

AVERY

We should talk, but you should roll through.

"Who is it?" Coop asks.

I sigh and flip my phone around so he can read the screen. He snickers.

"What?" I demand.

He shrugs again, feigning casual, and takes a swig of his beer. "Seems like she's coming around."

"Or Avery's inviting me—"

"When has Avery ever invited you to Thanksgiving? He knows you spend the holiday with your family. And you don't need an invitation, just like he doesn't need an invitation to come to Mom and Dad's for holiday dinners. Y'all have been friends too long. But, if you were going to dinner as someone's boyfriend, well, the protocol would be different." Cooper smirks like he's onto something big.

I roll my eyes and drain my beer.

AVERY

Don't give up on my sister yet.

And don't tell her I told you that.

I reread his messages, trying to make sense of them.

"Give her time," Cooper advises again. Then, he grabs my empty bottles and relocates inside his house.

I sit on the porch for a long time, waiting for dusk to fade into night. The moon appears, big and full and watchful.

Enchanting like the moonlight that streamed into our room at the ski chalet. That night, it washed Raia in magic.

My chest aches and I heave a sigh.

I don't want to say goodbye to Raia. I don't want to let her go.

And I don't want to give her any more time either.

TWENTY-SIX
RAIA

I AM thankful for a lot of things this year.

I am grateful for how quickly my body healed after my injury. Especially given the life-changing phone call I received from the owner of the Chicago Tornados last night.

I am thankful for my friends who still have my back and my family for welcoming me home with open arms.

And, I'm filled with gratitude for the time I spent with Cohen. For the gifts he gave me. For the love he showed me.

Want to know what I'm not thankful for?

This Thanksgiving dinner. Because I'm sitting across from Brooks and Anna, and it's awkward as fuck. This time, Cohen isn't by my side. Without him and the secret bliss we shared, my anger toward Anna, Brooks, and the entire situation vamps up.

We got this. I got you.

Cohen's voice echoes in my mind, and the backs of my eyes sting.

Unlike at the ski chalet, I'm on my own. Right now, I'm mad at Anna and Brooks for th too.

"Oh, the turkey smells d ous," Aunt Karen, Anna's mom, gushes.

"Gotta love a good turkey," Uncle Jim tacks on. I can tell he's uncomfortable by the way he looks away every time our eyes meet. Not that he'll say it, but Uncle Jim was never Brooks's biggest fan. Not when I dated him, and certainly not now.

"I hope it's moist," Aunt Karen continues.

Dad rolls his eyes at the head of the table. Avery hides his snicker in his fist. Mom gives them a scolding look and sets the turkey down in the center of the table.

"Dinner looks delicious, Mom," I say, meaning it. I haven't been home for Thanksgiving in years. This spread, this day, with my family, wraps me in a secure hug I didn't know I needed. In fact, a part of me craves it.

"Thanks, Rai." Mom beams as she slides into her seat.

"Where's Cohen?" Aunt Karen asks, beaming at me. "We heard he doted on you at the chalet."

Across from me, Brooks straightens, and Anna's eyes widen.

"He did," I agree. "Unlike this guy." I gesture toward Brooks. "Brooks was never a doter. More of a taker."

Dad chokes on his wine.

"Zing," Avery mutters.

"We should've seen that coming," Uncle Jim muses. I'm not sure if he means Cohen and me dating, or my comment. He lets his statement hang in the air for an uncomfortable second before he continues. "That boy was always around." He glances at Avery, who is trying to stifle his laughter. "And I doubt it was because of your friendship." His eyes dart in my direction, then away.

I appreciate his support, even if I don't know how to react.

So, I take a gulp of wine.

"Cohen's not feeling great," Avery fibs, covering for me.

I give him an appreciative smile and he winks. For a second, it's like we have our own inside jokes. Secrets. For years, that connection was customary for Anna and me. We could hold a conversation through a series of eye movements and facial expressions.

It feels good to share that with Avery. It's cool of him to stick up for me.

"Too bad," Aunt Karen clucks. "I was looking forward to seeing him. To seeing you two together." She smiles at me.

"Shall we begin?" Mom interjects, recentering the conversation.

"Aren't we going to go around the table and say what we're most thankful for?" Anna asks, trying to catch my eye.

I sigh. This was another one of our traditions. We used to love making our family members share the highlights of their year.

I polish off my wine. Dad leans over and refills it without commenting.

My blood warms and I meet my cousin's eyes. "Are you grateful for my forgiveness after you stabbed me in the back?"

"Damn, Raia," Avery mutters.

Anna sputters. Her mouth opens and closes several times, but no words come out. Brooks glares at me, but he doesn't stick up for her either.

Disappointed, I take another sip of my wine.

"I thought you said the air was cleared," Anna finally replies.

I shrug. "I was feeling generous at the ski chalet. Our friends were there. I was with Cohen. I didn't want to ruin the weekend for everyone."

"But you want to ruin Thanksgiving?" Brooks asks.

I smile spitefully at him. "I thought I was enhancing it. I can't wait to hear what you're thankful for."

"Let's say grace," Aunt Karen decides, her tone chiding.

"Sure," Avery agrees. "We could all use a little divine intervention right now."

Dad snorts. Mom blushes.

I take another gulp of wine before setting the glass down.

"What you should be most thankful for—" Dad says, pointing at Brooks. "—is that either of these talented young women"—he gestures between Anna and me—"ever gave you the time of day."

"Joe!" Mom hisses.

"I'll drink to that," Uncle Jim mutters.

"Oh, dear." Aunt Karen fans herself, flustered.

Anna turns beet red. Embarrassment washes over Brooks's face, but he doesn't reply. Does he ever stand up for anything? Or anyone? Even himself?

"Pussy," my brother mutters.

Anna grips Brooks's wrist.

I pick my wine glass back up and take another swig. For good measure.

I glance around the table. *Is this happening right now?*

I titter out a laugh, shaking my head in disbelief.

Are we seriously having a Thanksgiving Day showdown? With Dad and Uncle Jim at the helm?

I watch as Anna tries to smooth over the awkwardness. I don't jump in to help her. I don't do anything but sip my wine and watch the scene unfold. Like a bystander. As if this isn't my family, Brooks isn't my ex, and Anna didn't betray my confidence.

I watch and I drink, and I try not to laugh.

"Well," Anna cuts in. "I'm most thankful for Brooks, and the connection we have." She turns to look at her boyfriend. "I never expected—"

"I hope I'm not interrupting," Cohen says, appearing at the entrance to the dining room.

Cohen. Cohen's here?

I sputter on my wine.

Dad gives me another refill.

"Seriously, Joe? She's going to be drunk!" Mom hisses, darting to her feet.

"You earned it, kid," Dad murmurs.

I grip the stem of the glass hard enough to crack it.

"Cohen! We're so glad you could join us." Mom embraces him. "Here, I saved you a seat." She ushers him into a chair while Avery grabs another place setting. "I made the candied yams you love."

"And the turkey looks moist," Aunt Karen adds.

"You're feeling better?" Uncle Jim asks, leaning over to shake his hand.

Cohen stares at me, his expression unreadable. I can't blink. Can't speak.

What is he doing here?

What does he want me to say?

"I can't stay," Cohen says, holding up his hand to Mom as she sets a plate in front of him. "I just came to say something. To Raia." He looks at me again. His green eyes glint and his jaw is determined, his mouth set in a line.

He's focused. Committed. Diving in headfirst.

But this time, I want in on the freefall.

"Raia—" he starts.

"This year," I cut him off, "I'm grateful for my fake relationship with Cohen."

The table quiets. Everyone stares at me.

But I'm not nervous. I'm not on edge. I'm leaping.

Aunt Karen gasps, clutching her proverbial pearls. Uncle Jim looks dumbfounded. Anna and Brooks, surprised. Dad, truly bewildered and a touch angry.

Mom, relieved. Avery, proud.

And Cohen. Cohen stares at me in disbelief.

I take a sip of my wine for luck and continue. "Because it turned into the most meaningful, terrifying, exhilarating, and beautiful relationship I've ever had. Even when I didn't deserve it. I don't deserve you," I tell Cohen, shrugging one shoulder. "You were patient when I was reckless. You were understanding when I was uncertain. You had my back. You showed up for me big, Cohen. So big. I learned more about the type of relationship I want, about who I am, in a few fake weeks with you than I thought possible. I know I hurt you and I am so sorry. But Cohen Campbell, I've loved you since I was a kid. And now, I'm in love with you. Crazy in love with you. And I'm terrified. Because it's the most exhilarating and beautiful thing ever. I want you, Cohen. I want it all with you." Tears well in my eyes as I lay it all on the line. Every fear, every desire, spilled onto the Thanksgiving table with my family bearing witness.

I stand and the room spins as the wine rushes to my head. I shake it off and round the table to Cohen. He's staring at me in awe. Wide green eyes, a slightly parted mouth, and disbelief in his expression. I giggle before I dip my face and kiss him hard on the lips, proving the veracity of my words.

"Wait a minute," Aunt Karen whispers. "They weren't really dating?"

"Shh!" Uncle Jim hushes her.

"You faked it?" Brooks asks.

Avery slow claps.

I pull back from Cohen and wait for his response.

"You mean it?" he asks, his eyes locked with mine.

"Every word," I promise.

Cohen smiles and it's breathtaking. Relief swims in my veins and I kiss him again.

"Well, good," Cohen chuckles.

Avery snorts. Mom sniffles.

"Because I came here to say that I am so goddamn grateful for you, little Raia Callaway."

"Language," Aunt Karen reminds him.

"Shh!" Anna hisses.

"And I'm done waiting. We're supposed to be together. For real. For keeps. And I came here to tell you that I'm not walking away." He grins. "You beat me to it."

"Because I always win," I remind him.

He laughs. "Yeah, champ. You do."

"Get him a glass," Dad tells Avery.

Avery holds out a wine glass that Dad fills.

"A toast," Dad says, lifting his wine glass. Mom passes me mine and everyone at the table raises their glasses. "To family. To friends. To sticking together during hard times. This hasn't been an easy year for this family." He looks pointedly at Brooks. "But we're all here today to show our thanks for our many blessings. And to move forward, into a new season, with gratitude and grace for hard lessons and new beginnings. Happy Thanksgiving, y'all."

"Happy Thanksgiving!" we echo, clinking our glasses.

I finish my glass.

Dad shakes his head and points at me. "You're cut off."

I chuckle.

He glances at Cohen. "She's your problem tonight."

He grins and winks at me.

Avery groans dramatically.

"That was a beautiful toast, Joe," Mom admits.

"Well said," Uncle Jim concurs.

Anna smiles at me. I smile back.

"Consider the air officially cleared," I say, meaning it.

We got this. I got you.

TWENTY-SEVEN
COHEN

"UGH, HOW MANY DISHES ARE THERE?" Raia mutters, rinsing another plate.

She passes it to me, and I dry it. "You're lucky I love you, Raia Callaway."

"What? You wouldn't do cleanup duty for anyone?" she jokes.

"Just you," I admit. "You know, cleanup duty isn't a terrible punishment considering how many people we lied to."

"I guess," she admits.

"It's not that you lied," Dad counters, entering the kitchen. "It's that you lied to *me*." He gives Raia a look. "I mean, you told your mother and Avery the truth before *me*. I thought I was your favorite, kid."

Raia chuckles and walks across the kitchen to kiss her father's cheek. He wraps her in a hug and holds her close. "You are," she admits.

"Yeah, yeah. That silverware better sparkle," he jokes. "Your mother and I are headed to the Campbells for a nightcap."

I raise a surprised eyebrow, and Raia sputters.

Mr. C laughs heartily, happy to catch us off guard. "See? I can keep y'all on your toes too. Have a good night, kids."

Mrs. C beams from the kitchen entrance. She points to the island where a pastry box sits. "There's another pumpkin pie for you guys. Enjoy!"

Then, she and Mr. C head out for drinks at my parents' house.

"Weird." I shake my head.

"The good news is they're clearly happy about our relationship," Raia points out.

"True," I agree. "We'll never have to go through that awkward meet-the-parents phase."

"Today was awkward enough," Raia admits.

"Man, your dad was hilarious."

"You should've seen him before you came."

"Oh, I heard him put Brooks in his place. He deserved it."

"Yeah. He did. And Uncle Jim came down on Brooks too," Raia admits.

"See? There are more people in your corner than you realized."

"That's my fault," she admits. "I was so busy comparing myself to Avery, I didn't realize I was the only person doing that."

I wrap an arm around her shoulders and kiss her head. "It's good to have you home, champ."

"Yeah. I'm happy to be here, too."

I stack the final plate. "And I know we have a lot to figure out. But, if you play in Spain, I can come for a few months after the season. We can make this work."

Raia bites her bottom lip and stares at me.

"What?" I ask, a bundle of nerves forming in the center of my chest.

"I just found out last night," she says slowly.

"Found out what?" I cut in.

Raia grins. "I was offered a starting position with Chicago

for next season." She squeals and catapults herself into my arms. "Can you believe it?"

"What?" I sputter. "Seriously? Hell yeah, I can believe it!" I hold her close and kiss her temple. "You earned that, baby. I'm so damn proud of you."

She pulls back and smiles. "I can't believe it! I never thought it would happen."

"Playing professional soccer?"

"Yeah. It's been my dream for so long. I move to Chicago in January."

"I can't wait to watch you play. I'll be at every game I can make," I promise. "But, Rai, are you sure you don't want Europe?"

Slowly, she shakes her head. "Not anymore. The end goal was always to play in the States."

"After Europe," I remind her.

"Goals change. Dreams evolve." She laces her fingers with mine and gives a squeeze. "Now, everything I want is right here."

I kiss her lightly. "You want to get out of here?"

"And go back to your condo, where none of our parents will show up? Yes, please."

I chuckle. Raia swipes the pie off the kitchen island and turns off the lights.

"We're taking the pie?"

"We'll need nourishment afterwards..." She shakes her ass.

"Oh, you want to go all in tonight?" I tease.

"It's been too long, Cohen," she gives it right back. "I have needs, you know?"

"Yeah, champ. And I plan to take care of every single one of them."

Raia wags her eyebrows. "I'm counting on it. Let's go."

I follow her out of her house, and we drive to my condo,

our conversation comfortable and natural. It's as if the past few days never happened.

Raia and I are in sync. We leaped together, in unison.

When we arrive at my place, we discard the pie on my kitchen table and beeline for my bedroom.

"I missed this." Raia holds her arms over her head so I can peel off her sweater.

"Missed you," I reply, dropping my mouth to the side of her neck.

"This is the best Thanksgiving I've ever had," she whispers, her hands on the waistband of my jeans.

"Yeah," I agree. I tug on her ponytail until her face meets mine. I stare into her beautiful gray eyes and press a deep, soulful kiss to her lips. "I'm thankful for you, Raia."

"Me too, Cohen. I love you."

I grin. "Say it again."

She pushes my jeans down my legs, and I kick them off.

"I love you so damn much, Cohen Campbell," she pants, seductively untying her skirt and discarding it. "Now make me come."

I laugh and lift her, my hands palming her ass. "How many times?"

She chuckles as we drop into the center of my bed. "Three."

"You can do better," I chide.

"Four? No way."

"I like a challenge, champ." I unhook her bra and drag my hand over her creamy, perky breasts.

"Tell me about it." She points at herself.

"That's why we're such a great couple. We'll never tire of one-upping each other."

Raia snorts and wraps her legs around my waist, dragging me over her frame. "I love having you as my boyfriend, Cohen."

"Good. 'Cause I'm gonna show you just how much I love being your man, Rai." I kiss her hard. Then, I get to work.

And yeah, we make it to number four.

Thankful, grateful, and sated, I fall asleep with Raia Callaway in my arms.

Happy Thanksgiving, y'all.

EPILOGUE
RAIA

Three Months Later

MY HAND CLUTCHES Mom's as we huddle together, our eyes trained on the field. My heart is in my throat as I bounce up and down.

"This is it. This is it," Mom chants to herself, squeezing my fingers.

On the field, the Knoxville Coyotes line up for the final play of the game.

Of the *Super Bowl*.

There's less than a minute on the clock. San Francisco is leading by three points and the Coyotes are on the forty-yard line. The stadium falls silent as a hush sweeps the stands.

"Come on, Avery," Mom mutters.

"Let's go, Cohen," I add. I squint, clocking my brother and my boyfriend.

Avery calls the play and Mom and I press closer together, erasing any space between us as the snap occurs. Avery protects the ball, dropping back two steps and scanning the field for an opening.

"Let's go, eighty-two!" I shout out.

Cohen runs down the field, spinning away from a cornerback.

Avery lets the ball fly and Mom gasps.

I suck in a breath, hold it in my lungs, and watch as the football spirals through the air. Cohen is steps from the end zone as the football arcs. The moment hangs, suspended in the air, as the crowd waits, open mouthed and wide eyed.

"Please," Mom whispers.

Cohen outstretches his arms and the football sails into his hands. The moment bursts and sound comes rushing back as the stadium erupts.

Cohen dances in the end zone. The crowd goes wild.

Talon makes the extra point.

Mom and I turn toward each other, jumping up and down, holding each other with tears streaming down our cheeks as we cheer.

Dad wraps us both in a hug as we huddle together. The emotional weight of the moment slams into us.

"They did it! They won!" Mom cries.

"They did it," I murmur, crushed against Dad's chest.

The crowd is deafening as the Knoxville Coyotes win the Superbowl. The Superbowl! Just like I predicted.

"Hell yeah!" I cheer as Cohen's parents, Cooper, and many of our friends surround my family and me. Cupping my hands around my mouth, I holler, "Way to go, eighty-two! You did it!"

Dad chuckles.

"And number seventeen!" I tack on for Avery.

"They can't hear you anyway," Dad offers.

"A good thing," I decide.

Beside me, Anna snorts and bumps her hip against mine.

Our relationship has come a long way in the past few months. While I doubt we'll reestablish the blind trust we used to enjoy, we're friendly again. We call each other on the phone, share stories, and laugh often.

Anna and Brooks broke up right before New Year's. I felt terrible to see my cousin devastated, but I think both she and Brooks realized their relationship was a comfortable kind of rebound. I predicted that too. Still, their breakup sent another shock of tremors through our friend group, but our tribe remained united.

In fact, the whole crew is coming to visit me in Chicago at the end of the month. That's another thing that's changed. I am now a resident of Illinois, although I make frequent trips home to Knoxville. To see my family. To cheer on my guy.

Amid the raucous noise, our group relocates to the locker room area. Cohen barrels out of the door, his eyes dialed in on me.

"I'm so proud of you!" I scream.

He grins that boyish smirk and scoops me into his arms, pressing a hard kiss to my lips.

"Did you see that touchdown?" Cohen mutters.

"Which one?" I toss back.

He laughs, giddy on the high of his win.

"You played well, eighty-two," I say, tightening my thighs around his torso.

"How well?" He nips at my ear.

"Jesus, get a goddamn room!" Avery yells, tapping my back.

"You'll see," I whisper. "I'll show you tonight."

Cohen's eyes light up. He pulls back and brushes his thumb over the ruby earrings he bought me for Christmas.

I laugh and let Cohen place me on my feet.

His family envelops him in congratulatory hugs, and I throw myself at Avery, then Jag, Gage, and Leo, showering them with well-deserved praise. The Rookie, West, freezes, looking like he's seen a ghost.

"Is he okay?" I nudge Avery. "He played one hell of a game."

Avery follows my line of sight and shrugs. "I don't know that woman."

"Well, West clearly does," I comment.

"Hm," Cohen murmurs. "I wonder what that's about."

Before we can draw conclusions, Avery is hoisted in the air, and the team starts to chant ego-inflating things about being the Pride and Joy of Southern Football.

But I'm cheesing so hard my cheeks ache. My brother deserves this moment. He worked for it; he earned it. So did Cohen and the rest of the Coyotes. I am incredibly proud to celebrate their victory.

Reporters mill about, grabbing the guys for interviews and sound bites.

"Cohen Campbell!" A popular sports journalist, Kiki, grins. "That was an incredible touchdown in the third."

"Thanks, Kiki," he replies, grinning broadly for the camera.

My guy is the ultimate charmer.

"You won the Super Bowl!" Kiki exclaims.

Cohen runs his hand through his curls and glances over at his team. "We sure did. One of the best feelings of my life."

"I bet. What's next for you?" she asks.

Cohen's eyes cut to mine, and he winks. "Well..." He pauses to tug me into his side. He drapes an arm around my shoulders and kisses the top of my head. "As of next month, you can catch me in Chicago. I'll be cheering on my girl, Raia Callaway, number seven, shameless plug, as she starts for the Chicago Tornados!"

Kiki beams at me. "Can't wait to see you in action, Raia. Congratulations on your win, Cohen. All the best to you both." She turns back to the camera and Cohen and I step away. "Well, there you have it, Cohen Campbell will be spending the off-season in the Windy City."

I laugh and look at Cohen. "You're really going to move to Chicago?"

"For as many days as I can," he confirms.

"I love you, Cohen."

"Love you more, champ." His eyes glimmer. "You thinking what I'm thinking?" His palm slips down to my ass, and he squeezes.

I snort. "Yes, but we're going out to celebrate with your team."

"Afterwards?" he presses.

I laugh again, swatting his hand away. "I already told you. Tonight. I'm gonna blow your—"

"No!" Avery interjects. "No more. I'm sending you my therapist's invoice. Please, just for tonight, can we stop with the PDA and celebrate?"

Cohen and I look at each other and burst out laughing.

"Yeah, Ave." I nod. "Let's go celebrate. Y'all won the Super Bowl!"

Cohen wraps his arms around me from behind and leans his chin on my shoulder. "But I won the jackpot."

"I give up." Avery tosses his arms in the air and saunters off.

I giggle as Cohen chuckles in my ear. "You and me both," I say.

He kisses my cheek and releases me. "It's me and you, champ."

I lace our fingers together and kiss the back of his hand. "You're my home, Cohen."

And it sure feels good to come home.

Thank you so much for reading Faked and Fumbled! I hope you adored Raia and Cohen and their happily-ever-after!

Want more Knoxville Coyotes Football? Desperate to know who spooked West Crawford at the end of the game?

Make sure you pre-order Surprised and Sacked, releasing February 5!

Plus, learn more about the characters you love in other series. Knoxville Coyotes Football overlaps with the Tennessee Thunderbolts and The Burnt Clovers Trilogy worlds. Happy reading, book lovers!

ACKNOWLEDGMENTS

I am so thrilled to be writing the Knoxville Coyotes Football series! I've been wanting to share Cohen and Avery and the rest of the team since penning Hot Shot's Mistake in the Tennessee Thunderbolts world. Then, I met Nova and West in The Burnt Clovers Trilogy and felt desperate to tell their story as well. That's how this series came to be and I am loving every second I spend with the Coyotes. I'm firmly planted in my football romance era!

But, none of this would have come together so seamlessly without the love, support, and honesty of the wonderful people I've met, collaborated with, and befriended from the book world.

To Amy Parsons, Becca Mysoor, Erica Russikoff, Virginia Carey, and Amber — thank you for your time, patience, and friendship and for weighing in with your honest insights!

To Sheila Dohmann and Melissa Panio-Peterson — I appreciate you both so much and feel lucky to work with such great friends!

To Kate Farlow at Y'all. That Graphic — I love everything you create! Thank you for bringing my vision to life and making these covers so perfect.

To Dani Sanchez at Wildfire Marketing — THANK YOU! Truly, from the bottom of my heart, thank you for everything you do for me and this community. And, I'd be lost without you constantly helping me "rework" my calendar!

All my love to the book bloggers, bookstagrammers, booktokkers, and book lovers for sharing the books, couples, and worlds you love! Thank you for your support.

To Tony — you're still and always will be my favorite cover model! Love you all the world and am so blessed to do life with you and our littles — A, R, + L. Always.

ALSO BY GINA AZZI

Saving My Soul

Healing My Heart

The Kane Brothers Series:

Rescuing Broken (Jax's Story)

Recovering Beauty (Carter's Story)

Reclaiming Brave (Denver's Story)

My Christmas Wish

(A Kane Family Christmas

+ *One Last Chance* FREE prequel)

Finding Love in Scotland Series:

My Christmas Wish

(A Kane Family Christmas

+ *One Last Chance* FREE prequel)

One Last Chance (Daisy and Finn)

This Time Around (Aaron and Everly)

One Great Love

The College Pact Series:

The Last First Game (Lila's Story)

Kiss Me Goodnight in Rome (Mia's Story)

All the While (Maura's Story)

Me + You (Emma's Story)

Standalone

Corner of Ocean and Bay